GRAY

GRAY

Pete Wentz

with James Montgomery

GALLERY BOOKS

New York London Toronto Sydney New Delhi

Gallery Books
A Division of Simon & Schuster, Inc.
1230 Avenue of the Americas
New York, NY 10020

First MTV Books/Gallery Books hardcover edition February 2013

GALLERY BOOKS and colophon are registered trademarks of Simon & Schuster, Inc.

For information about special discounts for bulk purchases, please contact Simon & Schuster Special Sales at 1-866-506-1949 or business@simonandschuster.com.

The Simon & Schuster Speakers Bureau can bring authors to your live event. For more information or to book an event contact the Simon & Schuster Speakers Bureau at 1-866-248-3049 or visit our website at www.simonspeakers.com.

Designed by Renata Di Biase

Manufactured in the United States of America

10 9 8 7 6 5

Library of Congress Cataloging-in-Publication Data
Wentz, Pete.
  Gray / Pete Wentz.—1st MTV Books/Gallery Books hardcover ed.
    p. cm.
  1. Rock musicians—Fiction. 2. Identity (Psychology)—Fiction. I. Title.
PS3623.E593G73   2013
813'.6—dc23   2012022881

ISBN 978-1-4165-6782-0
ISBN 978-1-4165-7036-3 (ebook)

TO: B.M.W. AND ANYONE WHO HAS EVER GOTTEN
LOST TO FIND THEMSELVES. . .

GRAY

1

Sometimes, late at night in the hotel room, after the lights have gone out and the mistakes have already been made, when it is heavy and silent and still, I lie awake and listen to my pulse on the pillow. It's the only way to get through this. "Let's start this at the end."

That's how it goes, like a feather on a drum, bristling and quick, barely there. It's a microscopic sound, elusive, somewhere between my earlobe and my neck—a matter of nanometers—and I almost have to strain myself to find it, closing my eyes and holding my breath . . . feeling for it without actually *feeling* for it, because the slightest movement disturbs the rhythm, makes the blood slosh around and the heart stutter, turns the whole thing into a giant *production,* which is precisely what you *don't* want in a situation like this, lying in the dark with someone next to you, in some city somewhere, unbearably sad, tethered to the leaden silence of moment, sinking into the darkness. I am an anchor for an anchor.

Because then the anxiety comes, or the guilt (usually

both), and I start to think that I'm living in the middle parts of *Great Expectations,* right before things go really wrong for Pip, and of course I'm Pip, because it's my tiny violin playing this one, because everything has to be about *me.* And that makes *me* angry, makes my head pound and my blood foam up and all I want to do is rip off the covers and *escape,* only it's my hotel room and there's really nowhere else I can go, and even if there were, it wouldn't make a difference because I'd just be running from myself, and you can't do that no matter how hard you try, and trying hard is what got you in this predicament in the first place.

And then there will be sweating and rolling, pitching fore and aft. Seasickness in a dry-docked vessel. I will probably vomit. I'm an insomniac, my mind works the night shift.

So you have to be careful when you're trying to find it. I've had years of practice at this point, so it's not that scary. I'm an old hand, a professional. I don't move, I don't breathe, and eventually, I hear it: the soft, muzzled beat of my pulse, against the pillow, *ffft ffft. ffft ffft.* I focus a bit—carefully—and it grows louder, firmer, until the sound fills the room, blocks out the world. *ffft ffft. ffft ffft.* There's something comforting about it, because it always sounds the same, no matter what city I'm in, no matter how far I've drifted from home. It beats in perfect biological rhythm, blood vessels and capillaries thumping in precise, sanguinary syncopation. My body is a metronome, keeping time for the universe, the maximal and the minimal. All of it. It makes me feel less alone. *ffft ffft.* I think of phrases like *cilia* and *eukaryotic,* stuff from science class, and I can feel my body slowing down. *ffft ffft.* I think of the planets and the veins of stars, stuff from movie theaters and planetariums, and I can feel my head lifting toward the heavens. *ffft ffft.* I think of sleep, for the first time in weeks.

And then, as if on cue, she wakes up, the stranger lying next to me. My insomnia isn't entirely my fault, after all. Strange, stranger.

She's got her chest pierced. It's gruesome. It's gorgeous. Even now, in the middle of the night, her black hair falls over her eyes just right. She sits up in bed and is fumbling for something. I feign sleep, but she knows me too well. She flips on the light, pulls her knees up to her chest, and lights a cigarette. Her smoke rings are wide and gray, almost big enough to climb into. Like life savers off the bow of a sinking ship. She's trying to tempt me now, or talk, and I'm really hoping it's the former, not the latter. Actually, who am I kidding? I don't want it to be either. Because this is a giant *production* now. This has all gone to hell.

"Hey," she whispers, brushing her hand on my shoulder, "are you awake?"

I hate her. Really I do.

Of course, hours ago, in the back room of a bar, this wasn't the case. She had on nosebleed heels, her knees and elbows were as sharp as knives, and that piercing. She was across the room, sitting on one of those black

3

leather couches they always have in rooms like this, ignoring the advances of the kind of guys that always find their way back here. Her knees were locked, keyless, and she looked at her hands the whole time, in a way that made it obvious that she was trying *not* to look at me. But she was. The hardest part of watching someone watching me is making it appear that I'm not watching.

It wasn't the case at the after-party, either, when we finally spoke, after a few hours of doing stupid, arbitrary avoidance maneuvers. Shifting glances, wan smiles, F-14 barrel rolls like in the movies. They were stupid and arbitrary because we both knew what we wanted out of this situation. We huddled in a dark corner, I made a joke, she laughed. It wasn't funny and her laugh was annoying. This is routine by now. I could bring this ship into port on autopilot, could go take a nap belowdecks. In fact, I probably do. My life is so fucking predictable, my nights even more so.

She's got a mound of red cocaine, cut with strawberry Quik. They're all only here because I am too.

The cocaine was largely symbolic. *Phenylethylamine (PEA), the chemical responsible for the swooning and feelings of adoration, is structurally similar to cocaine. However, when given the chance, many people choose cocaine over love.* I wouldn't say that's a bad choice. *The endorphins released during infatuation are similar to heroin. OxyContin, "the cuddling hormone," most often found in new mothers and newlyweds, is like ecstasy; every touch tingles.* I think I read that somewhere. *Love exists in powder. Love exists in pills.* We are all addicts.

My head is swirling when I pass her my hotel-room key, surreptitiously as if it were a promise. It's passed like taking the new communion. I whisper for her to go wait for me there, and she does. It will be more than an hour before I even leave the bar, mostly because I like the idea of her sitting there, back in my room, bee-stung knees on the bed, waiting. Maybe she'll go through my shit, take something. Maybe she'll rethink it all and leave. I don't care either way. My moral compass is spinning next to the magnet that is all of my desire.

When I finally get back to the room and open the door, she's sitting there, just as I'd imagined. Knees locked, elbows sharp, the piercing in her chest jumping slightly. She's nervous, doesn't know whether to stand as I approach her. We don't talk. My head is still whooshing, but everything's slower now, sludgier. I push her back on the bed, kiss her neck, make my way down to that piercing. Her knees unlock. You can pretty much imagine what happens from there.

But now, she wants to *talk,* sitting up against the headboard, knees drawn tight, smoking that cigarette. This is her confessional. She explains how she ran away to LA or was addicted to OxyContin or something. It's all the same to me—a fucking red flag emblazoned with the words DO NOT BECOME EMOTIONALLY INVOLVED WITH ME, and this bed is barely big enough for my own baggage. I ask her about her family because it seems to be the kind of question I am expected to ask. She tells me her mother is "a French whore." She says this as she's stubbing out her cigarette, showing the tattoo on her lower back. I don't know how I didn't notice it before. It's something written in French, in dagger-sharp script. I laugh, she doesn't.

5

"No, seriously, my mom is a fucking French whore," she says, looking at me with wide eyes, searching for some kind of response. She has rehearsed this, delivered that line in front of a mirror while she put on lipstick. I hate her. I don't know what she wants from me, so I just roll back over, feign sleep again. She sits there for what feels like an hour, knees up against her chest piercing, then she turns out the light. I don't know if she's asleep, but I hear her breathing in short, little sighs. I imagine her chest piercing rising and falling, like ancient Roman empires. I think about her mother, the French whore, who probably isn't anything of the sort. At least I hope she's not.

In the morning, as she's leaving, I get another look at the tattoo on her back. It reads JUSTE COMME MOI. Hours later, riding to somewhere else, I look up the translation. It means "just like me."

2

The bus crawls into Dallas, but it doesn't matter. All the skylines look the same now. It's raining again, because the rain clouds follow me wherever I go. As usual, I don't have an umbrella. Life. I am not prepared for any of this.

Yawn. Squint. Dark glasses. I hate the way the sky looks at me, as if it knows everything I've been up to. I sit up in my bunk, in my underwear and sunglasses, listen to the motor hum and the miles whistle away beneath my feet.

I imagine the bottom of the bus falling away, me hitting the ground running, burning north up 35, cutting east on 44 at Oklahoma City, rocketing across great distances, jumping onto 55 in St. Louis, just a blur now, a bottle rocket headed north, past Springfield, Peoria, Lexington, Chenoa, Pontiac; then Chicago looming large on the horizon, me headed right for the heart of it, now supersonic, Kedzie Ave, Ashland Ave, Chinatown flashing by, digging my heels into the asphalt, making sparks fly, skidding to a stop on Lake Shore Drive, standing there in my underwear and sunglasses, my heels cooling in the morning light. Maybe a scarf wrapped around my neck for warmth. Oh, what would they say about me then?

I laugh about this to myself. I am fucking crazy.

Anywhere, Texas. Everywhere, USA. I feel the same regardless. I am homesick all the time. I didn't sign up for this. It used to be simpler—you know far—far, but never *too far* from home, from Her. Now, everything is bigger. Stranger. We have money, but we don't ever need it. We don't pay covers. We don't stand in lines. We sleep through the days. I mostly think of vampires, which isn't quite the same, but they are the closest I can come. They gotta know something about the way we don't go to sleep until the sun comes up. Or maybe something about the marks I've got on my neck.

"What the fuck are you *doing*?" asks the Disaster, who is inexplicably awake (or, more accurately, hasn't yet gone to sleep). He's staring at me as if I were covered in blood or something, and I don't understand why, until I remember that I'm sitting in my underwear, legs dangling out from my bunk, with a pair of $300 sunglasses on my face.

"I couldn't sleep," I say, which is a pretty good explanation for all of my peculiarities. "What the fuck are *you* doing?"

"I *didn't* sleep," the Disaster enthuses (our lives have become so predictable). "I partied the whole way here. Everyone else is passed out. Let's go eat."

We call him the Disaster for all the reasons you'd expect. He's always looking for something to ruin. He is a man of few words . . . a man of action. He has no feelings of remorse, no regrets. He is everything I am not. He's pretty much my hero.

In the rare instances when the Disaster sleeps, he does it less than three feet away from me on the tour bus. He's always beating off, and he doesn't make any attempts to hide it, mostly because he doesn't care enough to. Right now, he's standing between the rows of bunks, swaying a bit as the bus pumps its brakes (or because he's kind of wasted). He's got on boxer shorts and a shirt that says COWGIRLS RIDE BETTER BAREBACK. I know he put it on just because we're in Dallas. Those are the kinds of things he thinks about. It's enough to make me laugh because I know later on tonight, after the show, he'll *still* be wearing it, and he'll use it as a pickup line.

The bus pulls in behind some arena named after an airline. It's ten in the morning, but already, kids are milling about, some playing it cool, barely looking up from their phones, some losing their minds. There's never an in-between with them (our lives have become so predictable), it's full throttle or nothing at all. I watch them through the tinted window of the bus, feeling guilty. Sometimes I feel like the fucking pied piper, only I'm leading them down a vermin hole. I never meant to be like this.

The Disaster looks at them too, only he's a talent scout. He spies a couple of prospects ("Tremendous upside potential" is how he puts it), spits, and heads to the bathroom. When he returns, he's got his skinny jeans tucked into a pair of cowboy boots. They're made of rattlesnakes. Of course they are. He looks at me

9

for approval, and I crack a smile. I pull on jeans and a hoodie—my uniform—and we make our way to the front of the bus. Out into the spotlight. Showtime.

Of course, it's never that simple, so we have to wait for our road manager to guide us from the bus to a waiting car. It's something like ninety feet, so, naturally, there's no way we could do it alone. This is a voyage fraught with peril, after all. The convoy is assembled in the front lounge of the bus—someone has poured a beer on the Xbox, I note—and we head out, swinging the bus door open with a shudder. The girls start screaming, jumping up and down as if something were inside them that their bodies just can't contain. They call my name over and over (the world is on a first-name basis with me).

We pile into a black SUV, the Disaster rolling down the window to wave good-bye to his pair of prospects. This hasn't gotten old to him yet, and it probably never will. The SUV pulls away from the arena, making its way through the maze of empty streets, exploring the canyon of skyscrapers. Downtowns are always amazing on week-end mornings, nothing but shadows and lonely newspaper bins, coffee shops with the chairs turned upside down on the tables. Ghostly. You can imagine it's after some meteor strike, after the humans have died out. You can imagine grass growing between the cracks of the sidewalks, vines swallowing skyscrapers. Or, at least I can.

Now we're in the "artistic" area of Dallas—you can tell by the vegan restaurants—and the SUV parks outside one of them, some place with bright graffiti on the awning, and we go inside. No one even raises an eyebrow at us.

They're all too cool to care who we are. It . . . it's kind of refreshing, actually.

We sit at a table near the window, and the Disaster leans back in his chair, folds his hands behind his head, and props those rattlesnake boots up on the table, knocking his knife and fork to the floor with a clatter. He lets out a huge groan and wonders aloud if it's too early to have a beer, which draws more than a few disapproving stares from the room. It's all MacBooks and expensive jeans, beards and disheveled hair in here. Trust-fund babies and graphic designers and aspiring novelists. This only emboldens the Disaster, and now he's letting out thunderous belches and scratching himself. It's devolution at work. Man back into monkey. I look out the window, wishing I were anyplace but here. I stare down at the menu, but I'm not even hungry.

Our waitress comes by, and suddenly there's no place else I'd rather be. Jesus, she's beautiful . . . black hair and big eyes, hips that peek out of her jeans. She's got a tiny piercing in her cheek too, just to let you know she likes a bit of pain as well. I bet she hates her father and reads Camus. Naturally, she's the kind of girl who doesn't give a shit about me at all, which only makes me want her more. I take off my sunglasses when I order. It's the polite thing to do.

She disappears with our order, and I know I didn't exactly win her over with my charms. It's over. The Disaster is talking loudly to the road manager about something—the *Stunt Rock* DVD, I think, which has become a favorite of his on this tour—and I do my best not to listen, my eyes drifting from table to table. These places are always the same no matter where you go. Same terrible artwork on the walls (it's always for sale), same soy milk, same tofu scrambles with stupid names. Like the people who eat here, these places like to think they're unique. They're not. There's a place exactly like this back home in Chicago, down on Clark Street, where we used to sit in one particular booth and order coffees (because we had no money) and sit there all night (because we had no place to be), much to the delight of the waitstaff. We were such little shits back then.

"And there's a fucking *wizard* in it, onstage, and he's blowing shit up the whole time," the Disaster is shouting. "You guys should *do* that."

I think he said it to me, but I'm not paying attention anymore. I'm thinking about Chicago. And getting back on my medication. But mostly I'm thinking of Her. I've been trying not to . . . it's because we're in this restaurant. We used to waste the night away in that place on Clark Street, just Her and I and two cups of coffee, still wrapped in our sweaters, the cold still tingling in our legs. We'd sit on the same side of the booth and hold hands under the table, watch the flurries of snow whip around on the street. Eventually, she'd have to go home and I'd walk Her outside, hold Her tight to keep Her warm. The buttons on one side of Her coat never snapped on the other side. They were for fashion, not function, she would tell me. Then she would kiss me and say something like "You're beautiful for a boy" and make me laugh, and I'd watch Her get into Her car and drive up Clark, take a right on Newport, and disappear. And I'd go back inside and finish both our cups of coffee, just because.

Now I am here in Dallas, eating something made out of tofu. I don't even remember what I ordered. The Disaster is hitting on our waitress, talking to her like an old plantation owner ("Why, hell-ooooo there, darlin'") even though we're in Texas. All the South is the same to him since he's, in theory, *Southern* himself. Our road manager is laughing so hard he's nearly crying. The Disaster can have her—the waitress, that is—I don't even care anymore. I never really did. She just reminded me of someone else. You can probably guess who.

We've been broken up for so long now, but I still feel as if I were cheating on Her all the time. My whole life is an affair. I owe it all to Her. Her. She made me, she put me here. We fought about that. We fought about a lot of things, but I still miss Her. She is Chicago to me, the humid summers and the lake-effect winters. When I'm homesick, it's for Her.

We pay our bill and leave, but not before the Disaster lets the waitress know that we're playing tonight at the arena named after the airline and if she wants to come and check out the show, she should just give him a call. He doesn't tell her that he's just a guitar tech. It doesn't matter, either. She's not going to call. The SUV makes its way back into the heart of Dallas, the skyscrapers growing larger by the second, until they swallow us whole. There is something intensely foreign about Texas, like secession is imminent. Or death. Both are definite possibilities.

I miss home again. I miss Her. It's impossible for me not to. Chicago won't let me go. I realize that I left my sunglasses back at the restaurant, but I don't care enough to go back and get them. Maybe she'll find them—the waitress—and think I left them for her or something. I decide that would be okay. In the front seat of the SUV, the Disaster is shouting about wizards again.

3

Now I'm back on the bus, alone. The light on my laptop pulses white on black, like Morse code, sending distress signals into the dark. This ship is obviously sinking. I'm thinking about that waitress, about how I should've tried harder. I'm thinking about getting back on my medication. But mostly, I'm thinking about the last time I saw Her. It didn't go well.

Her lips curl when she's talking about the Q. Her middle name begins with Q, but she's not like that, you know? She's regular. She's normal just like me. But Her lips still curl in the most exquisite way. You should see it in person. I'm not doing it justice. I call Her up because I want to hear Her lips cup the air around the receiver. I want Her to put the receiver to Her chest, so I can hear Her blood. I want to tell Her to build me a model of San Francisco, because I have a great idea for a disaster. I was drunk if you couldn't have guessed. She must be on Her computer because the phone just keeps ringing. She can't be bothered to pick it up. Right now I want to shoot those fucking Harvard kids who started Facebook in their dorm room.

I call Her up again, to tell Her to build a mini-version of San Jose for me to devastate. This time she answers and tells me she is on the phone long-distance with Her aunt. "I'll call you back," she promises. I want to kill every member of Her extended family.

I call Her up again because I want to go over the blue-prints for a miniature Atlanta because I crave catastrophe. I want to tell Her I am the new William Tecumseh Sherman. She would get the reference, I think. Like I said, I was pretty drunk. It goes right to voice mail. Right now I hate Her voice because it reminds me of how much I think about Her. The faker. And I can't stop thinking about Her. I miss Her lips curling around those Q's. I miss Her body. After a while, when one bounces back and forth between different hearts, nothing gets old. You never really have to mean anything to anyone. My intimacy problems are with the world.

Finally, a call. I pick Her up at Her apartment, even though I probably shouldn't be driving. Her eyes are blackened around the edges so much that she looks like a raccoon. They look permanently bruised. She's always the consummate victim. Her hair looks like rows of shark teeth, just jagged dye jobs on top of one another, running away from Her natural color. No one wants to be what they are. We drive around the city so she can alternate between smoking cigarettes and drinking coffee. We talk about the kids we hate just so we have something to talk about.

We're sitting on the edge of my bed now, in my apartment. Every single inch on Her body is filled with millions of nerves. Somewhere inside Her brain neurons have fired to synapses and put them on alert. When my hands brush Hers, it feels electric. Every movement has a meaning, either yes or no. It's getting later and later.

The conversation and the possibilities are running out. Last call. Every time she moves Her hand to Her hair, she is sending me signals—fight or flight. Why can't I figure them out? Don't strike first. Wait until I'm tired enough to make a move. Lean in to kiss Her, bringing an awkward break in conversation. As I pull back, she keeps talking about writers she thinks will make Her look cooler. She's changed, I think. Or maybe I have. There's too much distance between us now to tell. Too much water under the bridge. Too much mileage between the legs. It's awful.

I push my tongue into Her mouth to kill the conversation. She smells like stale cigarettes, smoked by boys who were me on nights before. This is all I can think about as we begin undressing one another, panting with false ferocity. It's all a show, and we both know it. Her body feels hollow. I push on anyway.

Afterward, we lie in my bed, and I trace my finger down the scar on Her back. It runs the length of Her spine, as if somebody tried to steal it. I joke at Her like this: "Someone must have ignored the blueprints, look at all the structural damage." But I stutter and trail off. The smoke curls off Her lips. For a second, I am dying to be it. Dying to be as clever and kissable as Her. There she is, lying in front of me, smoking a cigarette, thinking of something or someone else. And that's how she is stuck in my mind forever. We are two explorers in the dark. Mapless and hopeless. Alone together.

It's funny how easy it is to sleep with someone, but how hard it is to sleep next to someone. It's too intimate. It makes my heart race and pound inside my chest. It's deafening. I slide my arm from behind Her head and slip out the door. I think I hear Her wake up, but I don't stop. It's summer in Chicago, there's a warm breeze on the street. Everything feels wrong. Street signs are watching me go over every moment in my head. Watching me remember Her. Mistake by mistake. Frame by frame. I'm not just taking trips down memory lane; I am broken down on it.

I am a corpse bored with my own funeral. I live like a gypsy, only with less gold and maybe more curses. People say I can't run away from my problems. I am the problem. Well, that's just shit because I've spent twenty-seven years on the run and can't remember most of the problems that started this. *Maybe that's been the problem all along.* It's funny.

It's late now. I've been gone for hours, probably, but who knows? I call Her on Her cell phone; she answers and asks me where I am. I don't really know. She asks why I left, and I don't know the answer to that, either. Or I can't tell Her. Same difference. So I don't say anything. The line is silent forever. Eventually, she tells me she took a cab back to Her apartment, says the door is unlocked. Then she asks me what the hell is wrong with me. I tell Her I don't know and she hangs up. I walk down to Lake

Shore. We used to sneak out of school and drive up here. I stand there for a bit, looking out at the water, at the darkened windows in Lake Point Tower. Then I go home. It's empty. A few hours later my road manager picks me up and we load up the bus and head back out on the road. I leave my medication on the kitchen counter, next to Her pack of cigarettes. Sometimes I like to think that they'll both be waiting for me when I get home.

One becomes a different person when they live on the road. You take for granted sleeping in the same bed, looking at the same clocks, waking up with a rug underneath your feet. The world looks different from the back of a rest stop. No matter how much you clean yourself, your clothes and your pillow never really get clean—and neither does your head. It never lets go of that smoky, cold/wet feeling. There's probably a name for what I'm feeling right now, but I can't think of it. I bet it sounds like Her name. At some point, I wanted Her innocence for my own. To breathe in every single breath that she breathed out; to taste Her spit; to feel Her falling asleep next to me; and know what it's like to be let down for the first time. And the hundredth.

I am still thinking of this when the guys all come crashing back onto the bus. They're all drunk, laughing about some girl or something. Someone falls down, something breaks. I pull the curtain closed on my bunk and listen. . . . I don't hear the Disaster, which means right now he's discovering if cowgirls really *do* ride better bareback. I bet he's still wearing his boots too.

Then there's even more crashing, and some cursing,

and the Disaster is aboard. He was taking a leak outside, for reasons clear only to him. I hear his boots clomping through the bus, back toward my bunk. He doesn't even ask if I'm awake, just whips back my curtain and turns on the light. He's wobbly, but determined. On a mission.

"You in herrre?" he shouts, looking right at me. "I've got somefing for you."

He thrusts out his massive fist, drops a pair of sunglasses on my chest. They're mine. The ones I left in the restaurant this morning.

"She came to the party, wanned to give these back to you." He belches. "She was asking where you were. You blew it, man."

He stomps back to the front of the bus. I just stare at the sunglasses, watch them rise and fall with every breath I take. Then I put them on. They smell like her. I pull my curtain closed and lie there for a while, thinking of the waitress, her hips grinding on mine. Just a little bit of pain. Camus. Her terrible father. I hear the engine start. We always slip out under the cover of darkness. Dallas disappears into the night.

4

"There's another trick. Here, I'll show you," she tells me. "Take a couple of seconds with each of the following lines. . . . No, I *promise* it will be worth it. Close your eyes. Imagine yourself walking down a road. Look around the road. What time of day is it? What does the road look like? Are there people on it? Do you feel safe?

"At the end of the road there is a ladder," she says seriously (she is majoring in psychology at Columbia). "What does the ladder look like? Is it made out of metal or wood? Is it sturdy? How tall is it? Would you feel safe climbing it? Next to the ladder, there is a box. What is the box made out of? How big is it? Is there anything inside of it? Is it open or closed? Where is it compared to the ladder?

"Picture a storm coming in over your head. It then clears away," she continues, really feeling it now. "Look up at the horizon. What do you see? Is it clear?" (I am grabbing at her now, but she pushes my hands away, pins my arms beneath her knees.)

"Go through this again and remember it like a movie," she says, giggling. "The road represents how you see your own life and the path you are taking. It's whether you see it as safe or dangerous and whether the people in it are good or bad. The ladder represents your relationships and friendships and whether they are strong and safe, and how important they are to you. The box represents how you see yourself, how strong you are and whether you are open or closed. Finally, the horizon represents how you see your future and whether you are hopeful or fearful."

This was the first time we were together, when the band was just starting, when everyone was young and didn't know any better. We were in my bedroom at my parents' place because I hadn't moved out yet. The bedroom is still exactly the same if you go there today. Same twin beds ("To keep the girls from staying over," my mom would joke), same posters on the wall, same window looking out onto the same street. Frozen in time. We had just met a few weeks ago. I saw Her standing alone by the jukebox—one of those giant, gold-plated numbers with the colored lights and the bubbling water in the frame (the whole situation was so clichéd)—wearing a hoodie, chewing on Her thumb, Her wide eyes dancing around the room. She looked like a fawn separated from Her mother, spindly and unsure, waiting to be hit in the dark by the car called me. She looked like a sure thing.

I remember walking up to Her and dropping some terrible line. She laughed, but not in the good way. I asked what Her name was, and she just sipped on Her drink.

She played it cool, just stared at me with those big, round eyes, yet to be blackened by mascara or life. It drove me wild. I remember the way I could feel my heart beating, as if it were up in my throat, and I remember thinking that I should probably just walk away. Imagine what my life would be like if I had?

But instead, I insisted. I pressed close to Her ear, begged Her, "Come on, just tell me your name." She laughed (in the good way this time), called me persistent, told me Her name.

I tell Her my name. I have just offered Her the first piece of me. Time stands still, the way it does during a car crash. Bent metal and busted glass. My words hang heavy in the air, spiraling in slow motion. Leaden. We have creased time, made a pocket and stepped inside. Her and I, enveloped and alone. All sound fades away, all the edges blur. Such is the case in moments like these.

"I like you," she says. "You're brave."

I'm not. I'm a total coward, only she doesn't know that yet. We watch the band finish their set, standing next to each other with our hands stuffed deep into our pockets, neither of us sure what to do or say next. Occasionally, we sway into one another, accidentally (but on purpose), and we laugh nervously. I steal a glance at Her in the dark of the club, watch those big eyes quiver slightly whenever the light shifts. She's concentrating hard, focused on the stage like a shipwrecked sailor scanning the horizon for rescue. She needs to be saved because she's afraid of what will happen next. I want to reach out and hold Her hand—it's such a simple, beautiful act, when you think about it—I

23

want to let Her know that she can let go of the horizon and sink to the bottom with me.

I notice so many things about Her in this instant, things that I will never find in anyone else on the planet: the way she bites Her lower lip, the freckles on Her nose, the curve of Her neck. She's amazing. I want to feel Her to make sure she's real. I want to possess Her. I feel my left hand moving from my pocket. It has a mind of its own and it's going in.

But then, the lights come on. Kids bump into us as they make their way to the door. Some red-faced kid spills a beer on my sneakers. Her roommate emerges from the crowd. The guys are standing back by the bar, and they're calling for me to go—there's a house party around the corner. Free beer and fistfights. I ask Her if she wants to go with us, say her roommate can come too (she knifes me with her eyes), and the games begin. Everyone who has ever interacted with anyone of the opposite sex knows exactly how this will turn out. There are politics at play, loyalties to obey. She will say no because she has to go home with Her roommate, and then I will ask Her for Her phone number, and she'll give it to me knowing that I'll probably never call Her, and I never will, and she'll swear off boys for a while, because we're all assholes, until she meets another guy just like me, and the whole cycle repeats itself, over and over, until she's lying on Her deathbed, closet stuffed with bridesmaid's dresses, totally alone and unloved, knowing that half the men in Chicago are walking around with Her number entered into their cell phones, and none of them thought enough of Her to ever call Her back.

That's how this is supposed to happen. Only, it doesn't. She says yes. Her roommate storms off in a huff, the first casualty in a war that will last for years. We grab coats and head out into the night. It's brutally cold, the wind tears right through us as we walk down Fullerton, and I offer Her my scarf. She says she doesn't want it, but I wrap it around Her head anyway. I wanted to protect Her from everything back then.

The party is typical: suburban kids getting urban drunk. Shitty couches. Stolen road signs. Loud punk rock is blasting through tinny speakers; you can hear the cones ripping with each note. They push hot air back into the room, make smoke rings with their vibrations. It's crowded and sweaty, and we lose our coats somewhere after the front door. The guys slip off into various corners of the room. She and I make our way into the kitchen, shouting to each other over the din. She's sitting next to me on the counter, Indian style. I lean in next to Her to hear Her words, and she pours them into my ear. I am getting drunk on them. Arms reach between us, opening the fridge, fumbling for lighters, but we don't notice. We don't stop. We're alone together now, surrounded by a million strangers.

She tells me she moved out of her parents' house a few weeks ago. Not because Her mom is a bitch or Her dad is a drunk or anything like that; Anya (that's Her roommate) just has a better Internet connection. I'm not sure if that's a joke, so I just go "Mmmm," take a drink of my beer. She's got me on the ropes. She has a younger sister. I tell Her I have a younger brother. She says she wants to go to Columbia next year; I say I already go there and maybe we can room together. She just goes "Mmmm" and takes a drink of Her beer. Maybe she didn't hear me. Things are getting critical now. Time to be bold.

"Hey, let's go outside for a second. I wanna smoke a cigarette."

"Why don't you just smoke in here?" she asks. "Everyone else is."

I make up some story about my asthma. I don't even have asthma. I don't smoke, either. She probably knows this, but I get up and she follows me. We push our way outside, and now we're standing on Fullerton again, without our coats. It's freezing.

"I didn't know you smoked," she says.

"I don't," I shoot back, and I grab Her tight. I pull Her close to me and we kiss. A sudden jolt goes through Her body, an icy bolt of shock, but then I feel Her shoulders go limp, feel the warmth push its way through Her body. She moves Her arms from Her sides and wraps them around my back. She moves Her left hand onto the back of my neck. Chicago does her worst, blows her hardest, but she can't pull us apart. She moans softly as I move my hand up Her back. I feel her soft skin run through my calloused fingers. It's so warm. I push Her against the frame of the door. Our tongues move in unison, giving pieces of ourselves to each other (imagine the possibilities of shared DNA). This could probably go further, right here on the street, but I don't let it. I pull away. We stare at each other, Her big eyes just happy slits, lips curled around Her teeth in some blissed-out grin. Neither of us cares that we're not wearing our coats.

I say something stupid like "*That* was nice," and she answers with something like "Yeah." Then we head back into the party, this time with Her hand in mine. No one is aware of what happened down on the street, that magical transference, that melding of spirit and body, but I have the proof right here in my hand, and I'm not letting go. I have a girlfriend now, with big, beautiful eyes and a neck like a swan's, perfection in a hoodie. And she's not letting go either.

Later—much later—she would tell me that she came to the bar that night hoping I would be there. When she saw me, she ditched Her roommate and stood right in front of me at the jukebox. She laughed when she told me all this, rolled right over in bed to shove it in my face. She had set the trap and I had snared my leg in it. Tried to chew it off. To be honest, none of it really bothered me all that much.

5

We are holding hands. We are having sex. We are each becoming the other. She wears my shirts. I wear Her. We are spending late nights sitting in booths, watching the wind whip down the street. Blow, wind, blow, we are safe and sound. We are holding each other in bed, I am stroking Her hair, she is falling asleep on my chest. We are buying each other used books at Quimby's (I am *The Nashville Sound: Bright Lights and Country Music,* 1970, featuring DeFord Bailey, the singing shoeshine boy; and John Wesley Ryles; and Charley Pride, "the first Negroe Country star." She is a tattered *Glory & Praise* song-book, with its Penitential Rites and such lines like "For love is stronger than death, stronger even than hell"—I underlined that bit). We are way symbolic. We are driving to the edge of the city and talking in vague-yet-resolute certainties about our dreams and our futures. We are leaving things in the medicine cabinet. We are falling in love.

This is the good part, the beginning, when everything is new and exciting, when every avenue is clear, every shop open, even though there is a parade in town. Life is endless, limitless. I haven't even thought about taking my medication in months; she is every pill I need. I am going in hard, I am putting it all on the table. I am casting off pieces of my past without hesitation. I am becoming who she wants me to be, even though she doesn't want me to do it. I am giving up the late nights; I am keeping my eyes forward on the street. I am saying good night to insomnia, saying good morning to the sun. I am everything I hated.

And what's more, I am writing new songs—better songs, the best I've ever made. "I love the way you have with words," she says, looking over my shoulder, but somehow replying "Thanks" after something like that just doesn't seem like thanks enough. I want to give each word a bit of vindication. But I don't, because each line is about Her, even if she doesn't know it yet. There is no magic formula, no deep well from which this flows. I am pouring my love for her into spiral-bound notebooks.

I could throw modesty Her way, but modesty never looked too good on either of us. So, I just nod my head absently. My pen was a life raft in the middle of the ocean, it was the only place I could ever be free. Grammar and punctuation were just someone else's ownership of my words, so I raged against them, blew through borders, made them mine. I would keep all my secrets inside parentheses. I would hold my breath before every period.

Now I'm writing Saturday-night words. I'm not dying with the words on the page, I am living *for* them. They give me strength. I don't worry about what will happen when the inspiration stops, because as long as I have Her, it never will.

We are in the studio now, a tiny space in a squat, corrugated office park outside Chicago. It's a by-the-hour kind of place, with egg cartons nailed to the walls, and a vending machine in the lounge that is never refilled (someone has written *Why bother?* over the Sunkist button). The matted carpet has cigarette burns, and the recording booth reeks like old coffee and powdered creamer. "The Bill W. smell" is what they call it.

I am sitting on the curb outside the studio now, watching cars idle at the stoplight. Their mufflers rattle, spitting out blue clouds of exhaust. Their wheel wells are caked with salt from the street. The drivers are wearing hats and scarves behind the wheel, smoking with the windows cracked. Someone is listening to the Bears game on the radio. Across the street in the 7-Eleven, the guy behind the corner is reading a magazine. I am pushing around puddles of slush with my sneakers, watching the tips get soaked, waiting for Her to call.

The snow is falling again, tiny flakes that flutter from the gray skies, land on the ground, and quickly disappear. I watch them stick to the arm of my coat, then blur away into nothing more than dark spots. Wet wool. I feel the flakes land on the back of my neck, melting, sliding down under my collar. I drop my feet squarely in an oily puddle, feel the icy slush ooze into the soles of my shoes. My socks get heavy with the dirty water. An old man emerges from an office across the parking lot, glances at me for a second as he lights up a cigarette, his hand shielding the flame from the falling snow. He pulls his coat tight and looks up at the sky, eyes squinting, then brings his head level with mine. We both stare at each other across the icy asphalt, me with my feet still in the middle of a puddle. A part of me thinks he's jealous.

The light changes again, and more cars huddle at the intersection, shivering, making the air heavy with exhaust. Piles of snow are on the sidewalk, the peaks black with dirt. The breath is steaming from my mouth, the snowflakes collect on my eyelashes. I feel my phone vibrate in my pocket, and I fish it out. It's Her. I answer it with "My feet are soaked!" and she laughs. I hop up out of the puddle, duck back under the awning. I listen to Her voice and watch the old man toss his cigarette onto the ground, coughing and spitting phlegm onto the ice. She's talking about Her exams as the cars rumble away from the light. The snow is starting to fall heavier and faster. It's beautiful. All of it. Everything is happening.

We finished the record just before Christmas, and right after, we shot the cover.

6

We have a new drummer now, a masher from Milwaukee. He's got more tattoos than the rest of us put together, is a militant, straight-edge vegan, and is always ready to fight because of that. He has a shock of red hair, and when he gets going behind the kit, he reminds us all of Animal, which is what we start calling him. Needless to say, our shows get a little more interesting.

Finally a major label has taken notice. We get a little bit of money from the deal, start to realize that, hey, maybe we really can make a living at this, so we decide to say good-bye to our ordinary lives once and for all. I drop out of Columbia one semester short of graduation. My parents are pissed. I'm not. I tell them someday they'll give me an honorary doctorate from the place, or at least spot me the twelve credits I need for my diploma. Those kinds of details seem trivial when your life is opening up, when the road is unfurling before you, when the future is yours for the taking.

There are, of course, roadblocks. When I tell Her that I'm leaving Columbia, she responds with silence. Then she asks, "But you're coming back, right?" I tell Her probably not, that the band is starting to do well and I was never really into political science anyway, so this is the right thing to do. I can tell right away that she doesn't believe me, and that, for the first time in our relationship, she has doubts . . . about me, about us, about the future. She didn't sign on to be the wife of a rock star, she didn't contemplate that she'd be left behind while I went off on my adventures. Most important, she thinks this is silly, some foolish children's crusade. She doesn't actually say any of this, but I can tell just by looking at Her that it's what she's thinking.

"What's wrong?" I ask Her, even though I already know the answer.

"No, nothing. I'm *happy* for you," she says, adding emphasis to take all joy out of the word. "It's just . . . I don't know, you know? Couldn't you just wait until you're finished at Columbia? I mean, it's only a couple of months, and maybe we could get a place together in the meantime, so when you come back, we can—"

"But I don't *want* to come back," I spit. "I don't ever want to come back here again. This place has nothing for me anymore."

It was probably the wrong thing to say. I didn't believe it anyway, but I didn't care. Something in the way Her voice sounded, something in Her tone, something in Her throat . . . I'm not sure *what* it was, but it signified doubt and had flipped a switch inside me. It made me want to hurt Her. So I swung for the fences, I let the uppercuts fly. I blew this entire issue out of proportion. Such is the way with these things.

"Oh, nothing, right, I forgot. I guess I'm nothing then, right?" Her voice wavered just a bit. "You think I want to just sit here and wait for you? You think I want to be your dutiful fucking girlfriend? You think I'm okay with doing that? That's fucking unbelievable."

This is going to be a disaster. The goddamn plane has crashed into the goddamn mountain.

"I thought you'd be happy for me," I mumble. "I thought—"

"That's right, you thought about you, not me. Not us," she fires back. "I'm really fucking happy for you. Is that what you want me to say? Okay then. I'm *really fucking happy for you*. Leave school, leave me here. I'm fine with it."

"You know, you can just come out and say you think this is a stupid idea," I say, for reasons unclear to pretty much *everyone*. "You can say you don't think I'm good enough to make it. Go ahead, I know it's what you're thinking anyway. And that's fucking bullshit, and it's not fair, because if this were you making this decision, I'd support it."

"But it's not me," she says, her voice trailing off. "It's you. And you wouldn't."

The air in Her bedroom is heavy with smoke, but the fireworks are over. We sit on opposite corners of Her bed, and she leans forward, burying Her face in Her hands. I watch Her shoulders rise and fall with each breath, first in slow, measured cycles, then building into more pronounced, irregular jerks. She begins sobbing, and there's nothing I can do to pull Her back to me, into my arms. Her face is flushed and the tears are pouring out of Her eyes so fast that I can't wipe them away, so I just sort of rock Her back and forth, kiss Her forehead. I want so badly to tell Her it's going to be all right, that I'll leave the band and forget this silly crusade. I want to tell Her that I am ready to settle for this life, that she is all I will ever need in the world, and that we'll never be apart. I want to tell Her that I will protect Her forever. But none of that would be the truth. So I don't say anything at all.

The silence is the worst part of any fight, because it's made up of all the things we *wish* we could say, if we only had the guts. And the unspoken truths here are plain: For the first time, I am thinking of *me* instead of *us*. For the first time, she is worried about our relationship, about whether it can survive the tyranny of distance (and what does that say about our relationship anyway?). And, for the first time, we're both wondering why we're doing this. It was a bad fight, it got out of hand quickly, and it was all my fault—seriously, go back and reread the transcript if you don't believe me—but it was by no means a *pointless* one. If anything, it was too pointed. This is how your heart gets snagged, like a balloon on a barbed-wire fence, this is where pieces of you get torn away.

Her roommate is washing dishes in the kitchen, clanging the pots and pans a bit *too* loudly, just so it's clear she's *not* paying attention to our fight. I hate her so much right now.

The tears have stopped flowing, and she sits up, sniffles a bit, rubs Her eyes with the heels of Her hands. She sighs. "How long will you be gone? Weeks? Months?"

I tell Her I don't know the answer to that, even though I do. The plan, we have been told, is to load back into the van next month, do a run of shows around the Midwest, then head directly off the road and into the studio. And we won't be recording in Chicago, either: The label has booked us into a studio in Madison, Wisconsin . . . a redbrick building owned and operated by the guy who produced Nirvana's *Nevermind* (they even recorded some of it there). It is going to cost money. It is going to take a while. It is not going to turn out the way she wants.

Let's just make it through tonight, worry about the rest later. I can see she is coming around now. I am pulling the wool over Her eyes. I am not the wolf or the sheep. I am another animal altogether. This is not dress-up.

"However long it is, I promise that when I come back, you and I will get a place together," I lie. "And, if you want to move somewhere else—if you really want to go to Berkeley like you've been saying—we'll go. Together. I promise."

Smart girls always want to go to Berkeley. Most of them never make it there.

"I love you," she says, sniffling again. "And I want you to be happy."

She cocks Her head and looks at me with those big, sad eyes, still red from the tears. She's waiting for me to say something. Anything. All that comes into my head is this bit of psychobabble she had once told me, back when we were first dating: *Freud suggests that in order to love someone else, one must love themselves; it's a classic "needs before other needs" argument. Unfortunately, no one really loves themselves. And, if they do, they need to get to know themselves better. Unfortunately, no one is really happy.*

Of course, I don't say any of that. Instead, I just mutter, "It will be okay. I promise," and I rest my head on Her shoulder. We sit that way for what seems like forever, in complete, exhausted silence, neither of us daring to let go of the other. Her roommate is washing the dishes. The radiator exhales with a dusty sigh. We fall asleep sitting up.

We leave for tour a couple of weeks later, on a cold, gray morning, the van and a tiny trailer loaded and rattling. Unsafe. I kiss Her good-bye, hold Her tight, promise to call when we get to Davenport. As we head west on 88, it occurs to me that she never actually said she was *okay* with any of this. We press on anyway, Dekalb and Dixon and Sterling fly by, ghost towns filled with sad people who settled for what life offered them. The road unfurls before us. Everything is possible. I feel sick to my stomach.

7

Des Moines. Van Meter. Neola. *I want to disappear with you forever.* Omaha. Percival. Sonora. *I want to run away with you and never return.* Kansas City. Bates City. Wright City. *I want to fold you and put you in my pocket and have you with me always.* St. Louis. Teutopolis. Indianapolis. *I don't know what else to say except I miss you and I love you.*

I write Her e-mails from the business centers of hotels. That's the reason they're there, after all. Sometimes we're even *staying* at the hotel in question, though usually not. Most times the person at the front desk takes pity on me, lets me type messages to Her without much harassment. One time, this woman at a Holiday Inn in Iowa eyed me up real good and asked me, "Son, are your parents staying at this hotel?" and I lied to her and said, "Yes," and then not only did she let me use the business center, but I got the free continental breakfast too. It was a highlight. It's usually just me and maybe some business guy in there —it *is* a business center after all—and he's always looking at sports or maybe reading some e-mails from his boss or wife or girlfriend his wife doesn't know about. There's always so much mystery in other people's lives.

I write Her e-mails because I'm no good on the phone. Never have been. And that's bad when you're out on tour, and the only time you have to talk is after shows, or while driving to the next city, crammed into a van with three other guys who haven't showered in a few days and make fun of everything you say. Needless to say, we haven't been speaking much. When we do, it's short, strange. A few minutes here and there, updates on Her classes and the latest drama with Her family. Tour is going good. I'm behaving. Gotta go, love you. We can't get off the phone fast enough. It's like talking to your aunt on Christmas morning, when all you want to do is dive into the mess underneath the tree. It feels like an obligation.

The funny thing is, when I'm not sneaking into business centers, I barely think about Her. There's no time. We are hitting the road *hard* this time out, something like twenty-five shows in thirty days, in big cities and college towns. We are sleeping on floors most nights, in people's apartments, and I wake up most mornings with my head next to a litter box. I have an uncanny knack for this, it seems. One time, I woke up damp with cat piss. It was another highlight.

I read something in a magazine today.
They did a study and found that countless men would choose

gambling over love if given the chance. Even more would choose pornography over love if given the chance. We are cavemen; and it seems like that will never change. I wonder if the men they studied have ever really been in love? I wonder how corporations will use this information to their advantage? "Hallmark cards and boxes of Fanny May chocolates will save humanity," or something to the effect. It depresses me to think about it.

I am writing Her an e-mail from a Super 8 hotel in Muncie, Indiana (they don't have continental breakfast, in case you were wondering), because I'm feeling guilty. Guilty for all the fun I've been having, guilty for the close calls I've had in darkened corners. Guilty for forgetting about Her and letting my life run free. Guilty for feeling good.

For whatever reason, it seems like we're against love. Everyone. People think love equates to weakness, or gullibility, or an unwillingness to deal with reality, so they try to ruin it, the social scientists and the admen, with studies and lingerie shows and boxes of candy. They try to invalidate it, dirty it up, but they can't, because people in love know the <u>truth</u>. They know love is good and pure and really the most beautiful thing in the world. They know love is greater than anything, greater even than <u>God</u>. At first, I didn't believe it, but I do now. You have made me realize it. Being away from you has been the hardest thing I have ever done. I am shaking and sweating. I am going into withdrawal. I <u>need</u> you. You are my withdrawal. You are my blood.

I want to protect you from all of this. When it's all over, I want to run away with you and never come back. I want to be buried in the ground with you. It's the only way we can keep this pure and beautiful, I'm afraid. We have to stay away from this whole life. We have to be normal. We have to get married and move to Berkeley. Our love can't survive like this, no matter how hard we try. I'm quitting the band. I'm coming home. I _need_ you.

I stare at the e-mail for a while, then I delete it. We'll be back in Chicago in a few days and she'll never know the difference. My conflicts of conscience are about the only battles I'm fighting these days, and I'm willing to fight until the end. There is something freeing about this life, about living out of a single backpack and disappearing into the night. About smelling terrible and never remembering people's names. About never having to say you're sorry. We exist outside of society. We stay up late and sleep even later. We are bandits, pirates, serial killers. The dregs. Someone should lock us up and never let us out again. But instead, they give us their money, they offer us their beds. We are not going to pay for the beer. We are not going to be back here for a good, long while. We have prior engagements. We have the money in a duffel bag. We have no shame. Fuck guilt. Back to life.

8

We are reunion sex. We are a freeze-dried wet dream. That's it, like an old song with a great chorus that never dies. Reunion sex is like Journey's "Don't Stop Believin'." It's like AC/DC's "Hells Bells," only with foreplay. The hits last forever. It's confidence. It's an ego boost. It's my best summer crammed into a stacked, five-foot-three-inch brunette. It's old hat. I know Her better than I know myself. I know Her better than anyone should know anyone, ever. I whisper this into Her ear, and she moans. I push all the right buttons, watch Her rib cage jut out as she gasps. The hits just keep on coming.

I'm only back in Chicago for the weekend. Come Monday, we're off to Madison to start work on the new album. But until then, we've decided that it would be best if neither of us left Her bedroom. We've turned it into a political endeavor: we're staging a Bed In, for love. We're a modern-day John and Yoko, and Her tiny apartment on the North Side is our Amsterdam Hilton. All we are saying is give love a chance. We will strum guitars and sing.

We will mail acorns to various heads of state. We might even invite members of the press, we're not sure yet.

We are joking about it, naked, wrapped in sheets and each other, when I realize that this is the happiest moment of my entire life. I want it to last forever. I want to be fixed, but, for the first time, it's not because I'm broken. I want to be fixed like a cat, so I never go and screw this up. She is all I could ever ask for, she is perfect, and right now, with those big, green eyes and pillowy lips and alabaster thighs, the idea of doing this for the rest of our lives doesn't seem all that daunting. She's the last reprieve. The stay of execution. She gives me hope.

But times are tough for dreamers. And even if my dream is a simple one—all I want is for Her to be in love with me forever—I know it's still a long shot. Life ruins everything. So I'm determined not to leave Her bed, because in here, life can't get at us. This is a restricted area. No trespassing. Which is why I don't tell Her about the parties and the girls and the notes stuck beneath the windshield wipers. I don't tell Her about feeling *alive* on the road . . . that's all life, the bad, dirty, savage kind. The kind I don't want spoiling this, the kind I have to keep separate from love. It's apples and oranges. Zoloft and Ativan. Church and State.

"What do you want?" I ask Her.

"I want this," she answers.

Exactly.

I'm a lifer, sweetheart, I'm here till the bitter end. I'm the floor covered in trash after the last dance, the remnants of the night that was. I'm real, I'm the tangible part of the memories. I'm the proof. You make me want to be this way. It would be easy to disappear into the darkness, to pile into myself and sail on to the next port. It would be easy to not give a fuck. But our love isn't easy because it's not meant to be. It requires work and sacrifice and protection. And I wouldn't want it any other way, not right now, with the morning sun making the curtains glow and Her arms around my neck and the sounds of the street so far away. I'm in it for the long haul, I'm not going away. Not until Monday, at least, when we must go on, when we are required to let life back in. Not because we want to, but because we *have* to. Life always wins.

"I don't want to go to Madison," I tell Her. "I don't want to leave you again."

"You don't *have* to go," she whispers, as she begins kissing my neck. "You can just stay here with me. Nobody knows you're here, not even the guys. You can disappear. We can hide out. Stay with me. . . ."

She keeps whispering *stay* as she kisses my body. She whispers it as she slides on top of me, wraps Her thighs around my waist. *Stay . . . Stay with me.* It's not fair, and she knows it. But I'm not going to object, at least not right now. She moves Her body up and down slowly, and things go electric. Neurons fire and pop. We play "More Than a Feeling" again. It's a great song.

After, we lie in Her bed and she asks me if I care if she smokes. I've only been gone for a month, and she's started smoking. It's because of school, she says. The stress. I laugh and tell Her I don't mind, even though I do. She fishes a Marlboro out of the pack, lights it up. I watch the smoke rise to the ceiling, drift over to a corner, and hide there. My mom smokes. The girls who hang around after shows smoke. The room feels different now, as if there were a window open, and life were pouring in through the crack. Things have already changed, just as I feared.

That's the problem with all of this. No matter how hard I try, I can't make it perfect. I can't keep it in a bottle, can't ignore reality. Chemicals are involved, the kind scientists try to synthesize and put into pill form, and they're making tremendous advances every day. They're winning the war against love. It's probably inevitable now. There are only two ways to see the world: either no one and nothing is connected to anything, or we are all a random series of carbon molecules connected to each other. Tell me if there's room for love in either of those scenarios.

I suppose there's no point in even trying anymore, so I let life back into our bed.

"I have to go, you know," I say, watching Her eyes for a reaction. "I can't stay here. We're booked in the studio and there's money involved and—"

"Oh, no, I know," she lies. "I was just kidding when I said you should stay. You can't *after all*."

She added emphasis to that last bit just to let me know how ridiculous she thinks it all is. Suddenly, life is lying between us. She rolls over and lights up another cigarette. Here we go.

"You can't just say something like that, it's not fair," I sputter. "I mean, do you think I *want* to leave you again? Do you think I *enjoy* doing this?"

"Of course you do," she sighs, blowing a column of smoke skyward. "Why else would you be doing it?"

"I'm doing it for us, for our future." I sit up. "I want to do this so I can take you away from here. So we can go to California and be together."

"That doesn't make any sense. How are we supposed to stay together if you're gone all the time." She laughs. "How are we ever going to move to California if you're not here to begin with? I mean, you're not even *living* here, really. You just blow into town from time to time. And that's *now*. What's going to happen six months from now? A year from now? Have you even *thought* about any of this?"

"Of course I have," I fire back. "I'm not an idiot."

I hadn't thought about it at all. Not even in the slightest bit. I have no plan, no idea of the big picture. It makes me feel incredibly stupid that I was willing to ignore the facts and put so much stock in something as pointless as love. Maybe the scientists and admen were right. Love is just something that can be made in a lab or put on a billboard. It has no practical place in life; it serves no function other than tying us up into knots, making us chase fantastic ideals such as "happiness" and "hope."

I end the Bed-In early. I'm a pretty lousy John Lennon. I take a shower, using Her shampoo because mine has mysteriously vanished. I was only gone for a month, and already she's making me disappear from Her life. The smoking, the shampoo . . . the signs are everywhere. I've just been too blind to notice them. I dry off using Her towel. Walk back into the bedroom and she's dressed too. I tell Her I'm going to go home for a bit, to see my parents. She doesn't object. We're drowning in life. As I leave Her apartment, I notice that my hair smells exactly like Hers now. She's following me everywhere.

I don't go home right away. Instead, I drive around Her neighborhood, make my way past the last remnants of the Cabrini-Green projects, drift through the Gold Coast, with its fortified mansions and luxury condos. I end up down on Lake Shore, as I always do. I park and walk down to the river, stare out at the skyscrapers, now iridescent in the sun. I'm trying to keep myself from feeling anchored or weighed down, trying to keep my mind off thinking about what kids like me deserve. *Desperation* isn't a strong enough word, but it will have to do. Life is going to get me. I've opened the box and let the Furies out. I dove into this headlong, went off to pursue this insane dream without so much as a map. I have no plan. I suppose it's only a matter of time now.

The best gamblers aren't the high-stakes players or the ones who can read the table. The best gamblers are those who know when to fold and walk away. Everybody gets it wrong. It's all cards and hearts. Everybody either gives up way too early or holds on way too long. I should've folded a long time ago. My wrists are only black-and-blue because I've never had the balls to go all the way. I've got ringing in my ears, but none on my fingers. I've got sunsets on the insides of my eyelids.

My phone buzzes in my pocket. Someone knows I'm back in town. I don't care enough to answer it, but I take it out of my pocket anyway. For a second, I think about tossing the phone into the river . . . maybe I could even get it to skip a few times before it sinks to the bottom and gets washed out into the Mississippi River. But I don't. I'm not sure why . . . maybe it's because I *need* a phone. You can't get through life without one. Any thoughts that you can are just fantasy.

I am torn. I don't know what to do. I've always been a dreamer, have always believed in the power of love and art and loud, life-affirming rock and roll, but, for the first time, I'm starting to have doubts. Can a dream even exist in reality? Or does it turn to stone the second it leaves your mind? I can still see Her standing on my front porch, hands in the pockets of Her coat, rocking back and forth in her Chucks. I can see every single blade of grass in my parents' lawn. Can smell everything in the air. I can remember Her jumping into my arms, saying, "Hiiii!"—and kissing me. That's the dream. The reality is today, right here on the shores of the Chicago River and upstairs in Her apartment on the North Side, in Her empty bed. You can't have it both ways. Everything has turned to stone, and it's all sinking. I can't even pretend it'll float down the Mississippi and end up in the Gulf of Mexico, either. I know it's too heavy, so it'll just sit there, down in the muck and darkness, with the skeletons and the sewage, probably forever. That's life, after all.

I don't know who to call or what to do, so I just stand there, by the river, as guys who have it all figured out jog by in Lycra leggings and tops with patented Dri-FIT technology. They said good-bye to their dreams a long time ago, they didn't dare to stand up against the current of life, and they're content. They're not the ones fantasizing about skipping cell phones off the surface of the river, or thinking about the blood pooling in their wrists, just below a thin layer of skin, just waiting to be taken up into the light. They're not the ones picturing the little blue Zolofts in their trembling hands. They have sex, not love. They have careers, not dreams. And they sleep soundly at night, they rise early and go jogging or throw on expensive suits. Sip coffee with confident, satisfied grins on their faces. Big board meeting today. Briefcases. Windsor knots.

There's nobody who thinks like us—Her and me—anymore. And it's probably for a good reason. We are dreamers. We worship love, we hope against hope and toss practicality out the window. We believe in magic and ghosts and lies. We wear each other's clothes. We huddle for warmth. We were made for fashion, not function. We have a lot of growing up to do.

And suddenly, I realize that I'm sweating. Or maybe crying. Or both. I haven't felt this way in years. I'm standing there shaking when I decide it's time to call my parents and tell them I'm back in town for the weekend. It's time to tell them that I'm crashing, and I need help. Call the doctors. Bring on the meds. If I'm going to limp through life, I might as well use a chemical crutch. Like I said, times are tough for dreamers.

9

The meds take two weeks to saturate my system. Even the US Postal Service works faster than that. In the meantime, I spend my days in the waiting room of my old psychiatrist, leafing through the same magazines, staring at the same framed print (a reproduction of Seurat's painting—the one from *Ferris Bueller's Day Off*—touting the 1984 Chicago Art Expo) on the wall. The waiting rooms of psychiatrists are the most depressing places on earth, and they're always identical, no matter where you go. Old magazines, leather couches, muted color schemes. Coatrack. Potted plant. Vaguely tribal sculpture/Persian area rug. Occasionally there is also one of those machines that replicates the sound of waves crashing or fills the room with the hushed fizz of white noise. The only thing that changes is the name of the city where the art expo has been held, but even then, the image behind the glass is always the same . . . Monet's *Water Lilies* or a Cézanne still life or van Gogh's *Starry Night* (because, hey, he was crazy too!), something swirly and soothing, meant to put the patients at ease, but instead just makes them want to rip the thing off the wall and smash it and slice their wrists open with the shards and get blood all over the sofa set. It's amazing to me that psychiatrists the world over haven't realized this yet.

At the far end of the waiting room is the door to the psychiatrist's inner sanctum, and behind it, someone is currently spilling his or her guts. As my session gets closer, there's a rush of anticipation, because I can't wait to see who will emerge from the room. It's usually a kid my age, and he never makes eye contact with me, just keeps his head down and beats a path to the exit. He's like one of those criminals you see on the news, trying to cover his face with his hands as he's being led away by the cops. I like to imagine what he's been talking about in there, what sins he's hiding, what's devouring him from the inside. I pretend that maybe he's more screwed up than me, and that, when I go into the room, the psychiatrist will look at me and crack a joke, something like "Boy, you think *you've* got problems," and we'd both laugh.

Today, though, it's a girl who comes out of the room, maybe a few years younger than me. She's got red hair pulled back tight on her head, and she's wearing a pink sweater. You can tell she's been crying. I turn my gaze to the Persian rug beneath my feet, pretend to be incredibly interested in the patterns of the thing, as she fumbles for her coat. I don't want to look up and see her face. I don't want to know what's devouring her insides. So I hold my breath and keep my head down until I hear her leave the office. There's a brief silence, some rustling of papers on the other side of the door, and then the psychiatrist emerges and asks if I'm ready. He doesn't skip a beat, doesn't even take a moment to compose himself. On to the next tragedy.

The psychiatrist is wearing khakis and a wool sweater. It looks itchy as hell. His neck gathers at the top of it, folds of pink flesh with a gigantic head perched on top. It makes him look like a snapping turtle. He sits back in his chair, crosses his left leg over his right, and asks me how I'm feeling. His pants are too short, and I stare at his white socks while I search for the correct answer. Fine, I tell him. I feel fine. Haven't felt anxious, haven't stood on the banks of any bodies of water and contemplated jumping in, haven't felt as if life were gripping me and squeezing the air from my lungs. I think the medication is working already, I tell him, even though we've both been down this road enough times to know that it's way too early for that to be happening. But, hey, there's no harm in trying to bluff my way through this entire process. He nods and scribbles something on his notepad.

"Now, the last time you were here, we were talking about . . ."

He says "we," but I did all of the talking. Psychiatry is bullshit. I know from experience. You sit there and talk and talk—about your feelings ("How does that make you *feel?*") and about your childhood ("You mentioned your *mother* there . . ."), about your fears and hopes and all of that jazz—because you just want the hour to be up, because you don't want to be sitting in an overstuffed chair in some stranger's office, looking at the carefully calligraphed diplomas he's hung on the wall behind his head, because you get the sinking suspicion that all of this is a gigantic waste of time.

But mostly, you want the hour to be up because at the end, the doc is gonna write you up that prescription, and everything will be okay. But the thing is, *he* knows that too, so he makes you *work* for it, just makes you keep talking and talking while he jots down notes and rests his head on his chin and tries to look interested. And if you're *not* talking, he'll just keep sitting there, staring at you, and the whole thing goes a whole lot slower, and you might not get your prescription at all, or, worse yet, he might refer you to *another* doctor, and then you have to start all over again. Like I said, I know from experience.

So, really, the best thing to do is just talk. After a while, you probably won't even know what you're talking about, you'll just be looking at those diplomas while your mouth runs on and on, and suddenly, you've said something you don't mean, and the psychiatrist will lean forward in his chair and say something like "*That . . . go with that,*" and you have no idea what *that* was, and all of a sudden you're rambling on about problems you didn't even know you had, or, worse yet, problems that didn't even exist until you made them up and spat them out of the hole in your face. And then you start freaking out because maybe you've just uncovered something *big,* dredged something out from deep within your soul, and now you're gonna be about fifteen times more screwed up that you were exactly one minute earlier.

But those moments never happen. I want to say

something that will blow his mind. I want great epiphanies. I want him to leap out of his chair and thrust his arms heavenward and go "That's *it!*" and pronounce me cured, or, if I say something really bad, I want him to drop his notepad and stare at me with wide eyes, his face going white as he stammers something all slow and drawn out like "What . . . did you say?" as he realizes that he's sitting in a room with the next Ted Bundy. I understand that's probably not how psychiatry works, but it would be nice every once in a while. Maybe I watch too many movies.

I'm thinking about all of this and muttering about something when he asks me what my girlfriend thinks about my seeing a psychiatrist. My mouth stops moving and my brain locks up. Panicked, I gather myself up in the chair, run my hands down my knees, cough a bit. I've been doing this for years, and I've never had a moment like this. Maybe it's an epiphany.

"She, uh . . . ," I stammer. "She's fine with it."

"You know, because she's studying psych at Columbia," he says. "We talked about Her in our last session, but it never occurred to me to ask what she *thinks* of all this. You say she's fine with it?"

This guy's good. He's actually been paying attention.

"The reason I ask now is because I wonder if *you're* fine with it too," he continues, failing to notice the gray matter of my brain that's now splattered all over the back wall of his office. "I'm interested. Do you ever feel like she's trying to pick your brain? Or maybe that you have to keep things from Her?"

He's really making me work for it now. I sort of hate him for it.

"Because, obviously, as we've talked about before, you feel close to Her. I believe you said"—he trails off, paging through his notes—"you said you've allowed Her to get closer to you than you've ever let anyone get before. So, your relationship with Her is important to you. And I'm wondering how that makes you *feel,* to have someone so close to you—someone you've let your guard down for—who might also be trying to get inside your head. Someone who—by your own admission—has such great power to, as you said, 'hurt you.' How does that make you *feel?*"

He motions to me with his hands, opens them flat, palms toward the ceiling. I hate when he does this because it's his way of trying to *draw* something out of me, when we both know that I'm just here for the drugs. But I oblige him because at least he's been paying attention. Taking notes even.

"Well, I—" is what comes out, followed by "No, I don't think that."

"I didn't ask what you *think* about it, I asked how you *feel.* There's a difference between the two." He scratches at his turtleneck with his pen. "I'm asking because I'm concerned that perhaps you have a challenge, and we all have challenges"—he never says *problems*—"but I'm concerned *your* issue is that you don't trust people. You *mistrust,* and in doing so, you create, uh, *challenges* for yourself . . . you feel like you must control every aspect of everything, you must try to keep things perfect at all times.

"And we both know that nothing is ever going to be perfect," he continues, downshifting his tone to Sympathetic Light. "We both know that we can't do everything alone, and that it's okay to *let people in*. Or, at least, we should know that. So, do you feel like you can't let Her in, because that would be giving up some of that control?"

"Yeah. I guess that's it."

"Well, that must be exhausting," he adds, ladling on the sympathy now. "I'm sorry to hear that."

I'll bet he is. We both sit there for what feels like ten minutes, just looking at each other. Then he does that motion with his hands again, and I officially mail it in. I'm not even listening to what I'm saying now, but if it's any consolation to him, I now actually feel *worse* than I did before. I believe this is what's known in the industry as "tearing down to build up." Psychiatry is a waste of time.

But at this exact moment, I can also feel my mind making a U-turn. Maybe this guy was right . . . maybe I do mistrust people. Maybe I am denying myself happiness and true love because of it. Maybe life *isn't* stacked against me, and everything can be okay if I'm willing to just *let* it be.

Mercifully, he glances down at his gold watch, sighs, "Well, our time is up for today," and is showing me the door before I even know what hit me. I don't even get a new prescription because he says the one he wrote me a week ago should be enough to get me through until the next time we talk. There's *always* a next time because psychiatry never fixes anything. It always needs a next time.

I walk back out into the waiting room, and sure

enough, some kid is sitting on the leather couch. We don't make eye contact at all. I grab my coat off the rack and bolt for the door. Soon, I am sitting behind the wheel of my car in a half-empty parking garage. I think about running a hose from the exhaust pipe. Then I reach into my coat pocket and shake out a couple of Ativans, the ones that look like Superman's logo, and I laugh for a second thinking of a dosed-up superhero ("Captain Lorazepam!"). I swallow them down and start the car. This time, there won't *be* a next time. The train is gathering steam, it's itching to leave the station. Next stop: Madison. Or madness. Whichever comes first.

10

I don't tell Her I've left. I'm not sure why. My phone vibrates every half hour or so, Her name flashing on the screen, but I let it go straight to voice mail. I listen to Her messages in the bathroom of the studio, away from the other guys, the tap running while I swallow my pills. As Her voice spills into my ear ("Hey . . . it's me . . . where *are* you?"), I stare at myself in the mirror and realize that I am nothing more than a smile with a heartbeat attached to it . . . skeletal, muscular, and circulatory systems, all color coded. Major veins and arteries. Major organs, easily removed. I am a living version of the Visible Man. You can see directly into me. I place an Ativan on my tongue, gulp it down with water from the tap. Watch now as it makes its way to my stomach. Follow it into my bloodstream. See it attach itself to the receptors in my brain. I'm here for your education.

After the first dozen messages, the *Hey*s get more panicked, and the *I love you*s become less frequent. She's worried about me, she says, and for whatever reason I don't seem to mind. I'm teaching Her a lesson . . . don't believe in me, and this is what you get. But then the Ativan rolls in over me like a warm fog, and my eyelids start to get heavy, and I start to feel *bad* for Her, so I decide it's time to return Her calls. She answers, and Her voice is filled with genuine relief ("Oh, thank *God!*"), but that quickly fades when I tell Her where I am. She asks me why I didn't call, and maybe it's the Ativan, but I tell Her the truth: I say I'm not really sure why.

I hear Her light up a cigarette on the other end of the phone, breathe out smoke with a gust. There's silence for a minute, then she asks when I'm coming home, and I say I don't know. A few weeks maybe. She asks me what I'm going to do about my medication, or my psychiatrist, and I tell Her I haven't thought about either of them. And that I don't care. She asks what's *wrong* with me, why am I acting like this, and I say I'm not sure. Then she says she has to go to class, and there's another minute of silence. I tell Her I'm sorry, but she just says, "Yeah," and hangs up. There's no *I love you,* just dead silence. I turn the tap off and walk back into the studio. I leave my phone sitting on the edge of the sink.

Here's how the next few weeks go: We start working on the album. We learn that while Nirvana recorded a bunch of songs for *Nevermind* in the studio we're in, just one actually ended up on the album ("Polly," in case you were wondering). We are bummed out by this. We take breaks from recording and walk down to Lake Monona, which is still frozen solid. We step out onto the surface, like little kids, and try to slide all the way to downtown. We attempt ice fishing, with little success.

We learn that Madison is a great town, especially if you like aging hippies and date-rapist/frat-guy types. The Animal tries to fight a group of the latter down on State Street. He punches one of them in the eye and it makes a sound like a water balloon bursting. There's blood on the icy sidewalk. He says the power of Dave Grohl compelled him to do it. We disappear into the night before the cops can show up.

We sleep on some chick's floor in the University of Wisconsin dorms. We have no money, so we survive on Fritos and Mountain Dew. But none of that matters. The album is humming along—for the first time, I'm getting my lyrics in the songs—and the music sounds big and shiny . . . like the way a *real* album should sound. We are becoming a *real* band. It doesn't matter that the temperature is in the single digits during the day, or that we are surrounded by burned-out professors and drunken bullies. In fact, that makes everything even *better*. We're a band of brothers . . . and we're out here alone, behind enemy lines. We know no one and don't need to apologize for our actions. We are fighting, we are laughing, we are alive again. Or at least I am.

Because the songs I'm writing now aren't love songs. They're *hate* songs. And they're all about Her. I want to punish Her for not believing in me or my band, I want Her to know that she hurt me. So I write songs—fantasies, I suppose—that put Her in the worst situations imaginable. I reveal high school shames and pull skeletons out of the closet. I spill secrets she told me in confidence. My pen is a weapon, and I use it to humiliate Her, to extract a measure of revenge. I don't use Her name at all, but when she hears these songs, she'll know *exactly* who they're about. It's awful, writing such terrible things about the person you love, but I'll take a pen and paper over a psychiatrist's chair any day of the week. This is my therapy. This has been building in me for a while.

One night, we're bored and decide to drive back to Chicago on a whim. Our producer doesn't think that's a particularly good idea, especially since it is around 2:00 a.m. and the dead of February in Wisconsin, but we keep pestering him, tell him we need to get a particular guitar, this one with great tone and so on and so on, and eventually he relents. We pile into his Mustang (an ironic one) because we had for some reason decided that our van wouldn't make it all the way down to Chicago. This was probably not exactly true, but, hey, we were rolling. We shoot our way down dark country roads, snow piled up high on either side of us, light posts whizzing by the headlights. We open the windows and feel the roar of the icy, black Wisconsin air; it stings our cheeks and makes our eyes water. The Mustang is slaloming down the roads now, slipping from side to side, the wheels frantically searching for traction. We latch onto the interstate in some place called Janesville, and the snow is starting to fall now, and everything is dark and quiet, except for when we overtake the occasional eighteen-wheeler, and we roar past its tires and you can hear the wet road passing beneath them with a hiss. It's slightly scary, to be honest: just one turn of the wheel . . . just one errant ice patch . . .

We limp into Chicago at around five, the sun not even a fully formed thought on the horizon, the city streets muffled by the snow. Our producer keeps the Mustang running as we trudge up to our practice space, our feet crunching beneath us, and grab the guitar (or *any* guitar). We all stand around in the room for a few extra minutes, partially because we're frozen from the cold— not to mention a little dazed from the trip down—but also because we want to make it seem like this trip was actually worth it. To further that cause, we decide that we should probably get something to eat, so we make the producer drive us over to the place down on Clark Street, where we pack ourselves into a corner booth, order coffees, and plow through tofu scrambles. The light outside is turning soft and purple; the occasional apartment window glows gauzy and incandescent. The city is coming to life.

Across the room is the booth where we shot the cover to our first album. It's empty now, but a year ago, we were packed in tight, Her on the other side of the table, looking at everyone but really only at me. We were just kids then. We're basically still kids now. Only I feel older somehow, more hollowed out. I didn't even call Her and tell Her we were coming back into town for the night. She's probably waking up right now, actually, thinking about some exam she's got today, or maybe kicking some stranger out of Her bed. I don't know why that thought entered my head, but it did.

We head back to Madison just as the sun is turning the skyline red, and no one is the wiser. The Mustang slides onto the interstate, the tires spinning through the melting ice. The sun rises red over our shoulders. It is quiet now, just the wind brushing by the windows and the hum of the engine. Everyone is tired, staring out at the rapidly widening horizons, the cities and smokestacks and scrap heaps giving way to barren, windswept fields, bales of hay wrapped in tarps, distant farmhouses, roofs frosted with snow. The sunlight is warm against our faces, our eyelids are heavy but happy. Good songs are on the radio. We sing along and pound the roof of the car with our fists. It's like a movie scene. Right now, she's probably walking out of Her apartment, sitting in Her car while the engine runs, blowing on Her hands. Unaware that I was in our city tonight, or that I made our producer drive by Her apartment as we left town. I'm pretty sure the other guys noticed.

When we arrive back in Madison, we sleep until late afternoon on the dorm-room floor, waking up when we hear the chick return from her classes. We walk down to the studio and get a crash course in business when we find out that our label has talked a major into giving us an advance to make our album. That gave the major the rights to first refusal, which was something none of us understood until later, when I called my dad and he told me that it meant that our album might actually come out *on* the major. That freaked us out until we realized we could probably use some of the advance to eat a little better, so almost immediately we start going out for proper meals. We ring up a bill fitting of major-label artists-in-waiting.

A week later, the recording is done and we pack up to head home. For the first time in forever, I'm not anxious to return. Her and I haven't been speaking all that much, and when we do, there's nothing to say. I don't know what will happen when I show up on Her doorstep tomorrow morning. I'm not sure who will answer the door. I sift through the pocket of my coat to find my Ativan. I fill my hands with water from the tap in the bathroom and swallow the pill. I feel the benzos enter my bloodstream, like tiny psychoactive snow flurries. I turn off the tap and shut off the bathroom light. This time, I take my phone with me, but I'm not really sure why.

11

Expect the unexpected. We jump right back into bed, we don't skip a beat. We make loud love while the sun rises on Chicago; we wake up Her roommate with the noise. When we're done, she falls asleep with Her body wrapped around me, and I listen to Her breathing, rhythmic and shallow. I feel Her body go still around mine. I let my eyes drift around the room: our clothes, tangled on the floor like the skins of ghosts; Her books, stacked on the desk—*Cognitive Psychiatry, Blackwater* by Kerstin Ekman ("one of Sweden's most prominent novelists"), *The Collected Works of Oscar Wilde,* bound in bright blue—proof of a life that continues on without me; an open pack of Marlboros, an overflowing ashtray, evidence of Her growing imperfections. The radiator hums away in the corner, and the midmorning light spills in around the curtain, casting the walls in a dull, white hue. Tibetan prayer flags hang from the light on the ceiling, fluttering slightly in the heat. It's like a photograph of a crime scene . . . *What went on here? Who where these people?*

Her cell phone lies on the table beside the bed, face-down, green light flashing. It's beckoning me to investigate, to pick it up and flip through the text messages and discover that she's been unfaithful, but I don't, not because I'm particularly trusting, but because I don't want to risk waking Her up. Instead, I bring the covers up to my nose slowly, smell them for evidence of transgressions—someone else's sweat in the fabric, some DNA left on the threads (I'm guessing it smells like bleach)—but all I can get off them is the scent of Her body. And cigarettes. It occurs to me that I might be going crazy.

"Why are you smelling my sheets?" I hear Her ask from behind my head.

As far as I know, there is no manual for moments like this, when you've been caught smelling your girlfriend's bedding for traces of a stranger's semen. No caddish article has ever been published on the subject in the pages of *GQ* or *Esquire* ("I was simply admiring the scent of the Egyptian cotton"), no father has ever pulled his son aside and explained how to get out of this situation ("Just tell her, Son . . . that you were blowing your nose"). The Smithsonian archives don't contain a single shard of Macedonian pottery depicting an instance like this. In fact, given the resources available to me, it's entirely possible that, since the dawn of time, no man has *ever* been caught doing something this stupid. Which makes me a pioneer, I suppose. So, in an inspired moment, with the winds of history at my back and the gazes of my forefathers fixed upon me, I do the one thing I'm confident they would tell me *not* to do: I apologize.

"Yeah, I'm sorry, I—"

It was a historic miscalculation. Somewhere in the Great Beyond, Abraham Lincoln cringes. From inside his golden sarcophagus, Alexander the Great slaps his forehead. Cain mutters to Abel, "Jesus, what's the matter with this kid?" I am an idiot for the ages.

She launches out of the bed, pulling the sheet with Her. She's shouting, *What the fuck is wrong with you?!* Her face gets redder and redder. Her entire body begins to shake, and great rivers of tears flow down Her cheeks, landing on the floor in a series of epic splashes. She wraps the sheet around Her naked body and begins sobbing, asking, *Why would you do that?! Don't you trust me?!* I just lie there in the bed, watching Her mouth move and Her body shake. The years drip away with each tear, the letters and *I love you*s are shaken loose with each convulsion, and suddenly I can't summon the energy to do this, not now, and not ever again. We are a dying star in its last cosmic throes. We are a ship with its hull pierced, the arctic water pouring in through the gash. It's over. Because the truth is, I didn't trust Her. I haven't for a while now, for about a million stupid reasons—the smoking and the moving of my shampoo, the overturned cell phone and the hurried long-distance calls, like there was somewhere she had to be or someone she had to be *with*—and one *real* reason, one that made me stop calling, and the one that had buried itself in my subconscious and had been gnawing away at my insides for months now: that she didn't believe in me.

In the end—and this was certainly *the end*—it wasn't

about who she was (or wasn't) fucking behind my back, it wasn't about the secrets she kept from me, it wasn't about the shampoo. It was something much deeper and more profound than all that. She had doubted my abilities and my dreams and my intentions. She looked at my life as a folly, a children's crusade. She didn't have faith in me to write the great rock-and-roll album of our time, to make art and save souls and, sure, maybe even get rich and famous and have hallways lined with platinum plaques. So she kept offering me alternatives—apartments and degrees and fucking Berkeley—when she knew I didn't want any of them, and she did it because she knew I would fail. She was certain of it, but didn't have the guts to tell me. Secretly, she probably hoped I'd crash and burn, come back to Her broken and ready to be put out to pasture. That was the breakdown. That was the disconnect. She didn't trust in me, so why should I trust Her?

My psychiatrist would tell me that I was projecting my insecurities onto Her, that I was frightened of success, but terrified of the alternative. That, subconsciously, I had doomed myself to fail, no matter what the outcome, so I was determined to control at least *one* aspect of my life: Her. Even if that meant pushing Her away, even if it meant denying myself the one thing that actually *made* me happy. He was probably right, but at this moment I didn't feel like listening. She was the fucking anchor that kept me tied to this town, to this life; she was dragging me down and she needed to be cut loose. So that's exactly what I did.

I probably could've done it differently, could've

explained everything to Her, or sighed that I just couldn't do this anymore, gathered my clothes, and left. But I've never been one to pass up a grand gesture. So as she stands there wrapped in a bedsheet, shaking and red-faced and betrayed, sobbing, *Why don't you trust me? What did I do?* I sit up in bed, grab Her phone off the table, and whip it across the room. It sails by Her head and shatters against the wall in a million triumphant little pieces, circuit boards and keys shining for an instant in the mid-morning light, then disappearing into the darkness. It was like a fireworks display.

She gasps and falls to the floor, sitting there for a second with a dumb look on Her face, like a baby who's tumbled over and is looking around the room for a sympathetic eye. Then she starts picking up the pieces of the phone, putting bits of glass and wire into a little pile in Her lap. She doesn't say a word, doesn't even look at me, just keeps gathering up the remnants of Her phone, combing through the slivers of plastic as if somewhere in there she'll find the reason this kid she loved so much has done something so cruel. Then, having found no answer, she starts to weep, and deep, seismic shudders seize Her body. She begins retching, making sickly, guttural noises that are broken up by panicked gasps for breath. She keeps muttering, *Why?*—but I don't answer Her because I don't know how to. I've broken us now. I know it. I am the feeling in Dorothy's house right before the tornado picked it up and dropped it on the witch. I am the buzzing and humming. The dog barking. The lady screaming.

I get up out of bed, pull on my clothes, and grab the

sheet off Her body, scattering the pieces of her phone everywhere. She looks up at me, almost in wonderment, Her eyes positively drunk on sorrow, and I laugh at Her vacant gaze. All we had left was fucking and fighting. And I didn't care enough about the former to keep doing the latter. So I did this instead. She wraps Her arms around Her naked body as I lean down, grab Her face with my hands, and whisper:

"Why? Why don't you call your boyfriend and ask why?"

I walk out of Her bedroom for the last time. I look back and see Her balled up on the floor, pulling the sheet over Her body. She looks like a victim. As I shut the door, she begins to wail, "Drop dead! Drop dead! Drop dead, you motherfucker," and for the first time in ages, I think we're pretty much on the same page. I don't slow down until I'm out of Her apartment and down on the street below. Businessmen and bike messengers pass me on the sidewalk, unaware of what just transpired above their heads. Cars idle at a nearby traffic light. I look up at Her window and realize that I've never done something so cruel in all of my life.

A few weeks later, the guys and I go to a house party on Kedzie. The second I walk in the door, I'm greeted by a hundred angry stares . . . obviously, word of my fireworks display has gotten out. I'm not welcome here, but I enter anyway. I haven't even shed my coat when I hear Her voice coming from the living room. She's drunk and shouting about something intellectual—"Aleister Crowley fucking *hated women,*" I think it was. I walk into the room and stand by the doorway, watch as she throws Her hands wildly in the air, spilling wine everywhere as she shouts about Crowley's "avowed anti-Semitism." She's seated on the arm of a sofa, Her feet resting in the lap of some bar-room philosopher, who's stroking Her back and laughing at Her brilliance. It only hurts a little when I see Her like this, but mostly I just feel sorry for Her. She's drunk and embarrassing Herself. She looks ridiculous.

She doesn't even notice me standing by the door, but the philosopher does, looking up from his bottled import, his eyes locking on mine. His buddies on the sofa see me too, and they puff their chests accordingly, a gang of wannabe rockabilly Dharma Bums with black-rimmed glasses and neck tattoos and cuffed jeans. I just smile and wink at them all. They look fucking ridiculous too.

A few minutes later, I'm down on Kedzie, bumming a cigarette from a girl (I smoke now too, by the way), when I get a forearm shoved into my back. My heart starts thumping and my face hurts before I can even turn around. I know what's coming next. In Chicago, if you hit somebody in the winter, you really mean it. I whirl around, cigarette dangling out of my mouth, and I'm greeted by my friend the philosopher. He says hello with his fists.

The first punch to my stomach turns my guts inside out. I fall onto the curb and hear my keys clink down the street. I spit up blood, steaming in the winter air, then, in a move of pure showmanship, I lick it off my hand and slap the philosopher in the face, then walk off to find my keys. He spins me around before he hits me again, I laugh 'cause my spit and blood on his face look like war paint. His rockabilly pals are down on the street now, inching closer to the fray but not willing to actually fight. Cowards.

Then the philosopher rears back and blasts me in the face, hits me dead center and tells me it's for Her, asks how I like being abused. I remember thinking that, for a bookish guy, he punches pretty well, and he's got a quick wit too. Then it all goes black. Getting punched in the face is like a hiccup in time, it all slows down from there. All of a sudden, every single tear duct in my head starts working overtime to get enough buckets out. The tears are freezing on my cheeks, and the blood starts caking on my face, mixing with the dirt of the Chicago street. I hear Converse pounding the cement in the distance; the sound is absolutely gorgeous. All I can do is crack a smile at this stupid kid—the kind of smile that says *too late*. Sound the cannons. The cavalry has arrived. This is why it's a good thing to have a guy like the Animal on your side.

He plows through the philosopher, knocking him to the street with a thud. In an instant, he's on top of him, pounding his face with his fists, calling him motherfucker and pussy and bitch. The philosopher can't even cover up, and now he's making gurgling noises. The Animal relents, mostly because he doesn't want to kill the kid, and the philosopher staggers off down the street. It only takes us a split second to start chasing after him, the Animal laughing like a maniac, breathing steam into the night air. We fly around a corner and the Animal catches his prey on the front porch of a row house, pulling him off it, the skin on the philosopher's hand tearing as he is wrenched from the safety of the doorknob he has anchored himself on.

He's screaming like he's being murdered. We're panting in the cold air. The Animal holds his prey as I start laying into him. Again and again. Right hand only. I want him to feel every hit. Blood starts pouring out of his mouth—no more witty words, motherfucker—and the porch light turns on. Out steps the philosopher's mom, a winter coat pulled over her shoulders. The Animal tells her, "Get back in the fucking house," and I start punctuating each shot I take with a "This is for your fucking mother." He's defiant until the end, I gotta give him that, no white flags, just "Fuck you" between every hit. But I get into a rhythm and eventually his body goes limp. The Animal lays him down in the snow, and then, with his mom looking on from the window, I stand over his body and spit my blood into his mouth.

We book it down the street and don't stop until we're practically standing in Lake Michigan. Hands on our hips, lungs aching for air, the Animal and I start laughing. He lived with his fucking *mother*. We wash the blood off our faces and hands in a pile of dirty snow, and the Animal tells me I should probably go to the emergency room. I want to go back and find my keys, but I defer to his better judgment. He knows a mortal wound when he sees one, after all.

We walk for ages, eventually finding a hospital. We stagger in, me holding a bloody snowball to my mouth, and I tell the girl behind the desk that I'm looking to trade in some broken knuckles for 20 cc of self-esteem. She said my plan probably wouldn't cover that. She's funny. Because I am concussed, I decide that I'm gonna try and call Her from the pay phone in the waiting room.

I drop a quarter and a dime into the slot, and start punching in Her number. I get about halfway through before I realize that she doesn't have a cell phone anymore because I smashed Her last one. I hang up the receiver and listen to the coins drop into the return. I don't pick them up. I spit some blood onto the linoleum floor and walk back to the ER to have my face reattached. Fucker.

12

My life goes supersonic.

We're selling tons of merch at each show, making real money now, but since we're still just the openers, the club owners don't pay much attention, which means we're able to give them a few hundred bucks each night and simply pocket the rest. They don't suspect a thing, mostly because this has never happened before. We eat actual dinners and stay in actual hotels and even consider getting an actual tour bus, but they run about thirty grand a month and we're not there just yet. But we're getting close. Like I said, it's really happening now.

The tour stretches on, the weeks become months, the shows get bigger and bigger, until finally, on the day our album is released, we return to Chicago for a homecoming show at the Metro. It's sold-out, absolutely packed, and backstage, in the cramped dressing room, with our parents looking on and bottles of champagne stuffed in a Styrofoam cooler, we meet with an A&R guy from the major label and sign our names on the dotted line. In an instant, our stupid little band becomes labelmates with the likes of Jay-Z and U-fucking-2. We pop the champagne and spray it around the room, the way the Bulls did during the Jordan era, and my mom even cries a little bit. It's the single most amazing moment of my life. I mean it. It has officially happened.

There's an actual after-party too, at an actual *bar* with an actual open tab. I am told by our A&R guy that this is our record-release party. Everyone in Chicago shows up to drink the free booze. Everyone except Her. She was probably studying or hanging out with the philosopher and his mom or something. It doesn't matter, really. I'm too buzzed to be sad about Her, too flushed with the present to think about the past. I tell myself this with every shot our A&R guy buys for me, and eventually, I actually believe it. Or I just get too drunk to care.

When they tell you not to drink alcohol or operate heavy machinery while taking Ativan, they're not kidding. I'm *amazingly* drunk at this point, stumbling around the bar, bumping into people, spilling drinks all over myself. I'm laughing like a lunatic, shouting in people's ears, yelling at the DJ to play some good music. I can't imagine what I would've done if they let me drive a forklift. People are staring at me sideways, whispering shit about me in dark corners, but I don't care. This is my party. Or my band's. Whatever.

At some point, I go into the bathroom and lock the door, stare at myself in the mirror, then proceed to puke all over the sink. It's red from all the liquor I've been drinking, or from blood. I remember how in *The Catcher in the Rye,* Holden Caulfield used to pretend he had been shot in the gut, used to clutch his stomach and grunt, "They got me . . . they got me good," so I do the same thing, stumbling around the bathroom, backing into the wall, sliding down, collapsing into an imaginary pool of my own blood. I'm a funny motherfucker when I'm drunk, I think to myself. Then I black out.

The next thing I remember, I'm in the backseat of a cab, headed somewhere with some scene chick I've never met before. I actually come to as we're making out, my tongue halfway down her throat, my hand halfway up her skirt. We paw and slobber for a few blocks, and every once in a while I catch the cabdriver watching us in the rearview mirror. Part of me wants to ask him for help, but I don't. Instead I just move my hand between her legs. We pull up outside her apartment, in a part of town I don't recognize. We grope each other as we head up her stairs, and then we're inside her place.

"I just want you to know that I never do things like this," she admits, but only people who always do things like this say lines like that. We are clumsy as we make our moves. As this stranger fumbles with my belt, I suddenly realize that this officially means it's over between Her and me. It's funny the things that cross my mind in moments like this. Depressing too. So I block it out and get to work. I pull at her buckle; it's turned around to the side of her pants. *Ten scene points.* I grab her hair, which is jet-black and covers her face in just the right way. *Twenty-five scene points.* She's about to get the boy you couldn't catch in between the sheets. *One hundred scene points.*

We grunt and sweat all over each other, her hair hanging like a black cloud over my head as I lie under her. She moans and wails as if she's just found religion, rolls her eyes back in her head, runs her nails down my back. It's all a big show. The thought crosses my mind that there's not much difference between fucking and a fistfight. At least not right now. It ends with her shouting, "Oh, God," over and over. Her poor roommates. We lie there drenched in sweat, white sheets clinging to our bodies. I'm starting to sober up now, and all I want to do is escape. So I make up a lie, say I have to get back to the van by 6:00 a.m. because we're heading out of town. I don't know if she believes me or not, and I don't care.

Her alarm goes off at 5:30 a.m., but we are both still awake. She walks me down to the street as I desperately scan the horizon for a cab. The air is heavy and damp with the impending promise of spring, and if I weren't standing out here with a complete stranger, wearing a shirt still covered in booze and what appears to be dried vomit, I'm sure I'd be enjoying this right now. Finally, I spot a cab and frantically wave it down ("Save me!"). As it pulls to the curb, she pulls my hand toward her, writes *Bastard* on it, then scribbles her number below that. I look at it for a second, then, not knowing what to do or say next, jump in the cab and tell the driver to go. We take a right, then another right, and another, and I doze off. I wake up as the cab comes to a stop in front of my parents' house. I'm not sure how he knew to stop here. I walk up the stairs and into my room, drop my clothes in a pile by the door, and am asleep by 6:00 a.m. I sweat out the booze, and by the time I wake up, her number has worn off my hand. But the *Bastard* is still there. I look at it and laugh, even though I'm probably not supposed to. The truth will do that to you.

It's way past noon when I finally crawl out of bed. I'm so hungover, I can't even see straight. My folks have decided to have mercy on me—they've left a pot of coffee on the burner and gone out for the afternoon. A year ago, they would've given me such shit for rolling in at 6:00 a.m., but now, things are different.

I sit in the kitchen while the rest of the world carries on without me. Somewhere someone is mowing a lawn. Somewhere someone is beeping a horn. My parents' dogs are going nuts about something in the backyard, but I'm too sick to get up and see what it is. I drink my coffee and move my eyes around the room . . . the bowl of fruit my mom is constantly refilling, mostly because the apples keep going bad. The wallpaper that my dad hated hanging, golden fleurs-de-lis entwined with fingers of ivy. The big, stainless-steel fridge, with a picture of my brother playing soccer and an old promo photo of my band (me with long hair too). I've been in this room a million times over the years, but it's never seemed as still and sad as it does in this moment. It's like sitting in the kitchen of someone who's just died. The cabinets are filled with cans they'll never open, the freezer stuffed with meat they'll never thaw. The air is heavy and you don't want to disturb anything because, you know, *that's the way they left it*. Maybe it's just because I'm hungover though.

I reach across the table and pull a stack of mail toward me. There are offers for credit cards, a newsletter from the Wilmette Public Library, and a letter from the Columbia Registrar's Office, addressed to me. I don't even open it, just rip it in half and toss it toward the garbage can. I miss by a mile, and the two halves of the envelope flutter harmlessly to the floor. I'll get them in a minute. I finish my coffee and put the mug in the sink, run some water for no particular reason. The dogs are chasing each other around the backyard, stopping, staring each other down, then bolting off again. I watch them through the kitchen window and smile. I can hear kids playing next door, making up simple games with infinitely complex rules ("You can't touch the grass because it's *lava,*"), and I can remember me and my brother doing the same thing. It seems like that was fifty years ago for some reason.

I stand there for a while, the water running, the kids burning up in the imaginary lava, and I start to think about Her. I wonder if she knows the girl I was with last night. I wonder if she'll even care? And I wonder if she thought about *me* the first time she had sex with the philosopher? Probably not. Then, out of nowhere, an overwhelming sadness comes over me, makes me shiver, and I decide to never come back to this house again. I decide I'm going to move far away from here, I'm going to hide and never come back. I turn off the tap, then throw up in the sink. It's still red. Probably from the blood.

13

The cities start to blur together. The shows do the same. The days are indefinable, and time is only marked by events: In May, we get a full-time publicist from the label. In June, we get a manager. In July, we say good-bye to the van and get a tour bus (which we're sharing with another band to cut costs . . . our manager wasted no time in proving his worth). The shower on the bus is like an old phone booth. The bunks are like coffins. None of this matters to me in the slightest. We've been out on the road for months now, living out of duffel bags, washing ourselves with tiny bars of soap pilfered from hotel supply rooms, sleeping when the sun comes up, and none of that matters to me, either. Every day is a new adventure, every city a new opportunity.

After a show in Las Vegas (I think it was Las Vegas) I meet an actress who used to be on a show I watched as a kid, and we hit it off. She is drinking whatever lowers her standards and laughing at all my jokes and touching my knee with her hand. She's got downtown legs that are too tall for every single pair of pants she owns. People would pay to have problems like that. She looks at my eyes, darkened around the edges, and I can tell it gets her going because she thinks I can relate to her troubles. She doesn't know I've always been this way; that I'm just a rainy day kid and have been from the start. Or, she doesn't care.

She asks to see our bus. I take her on, and before I know it, she's sliding into my bunk. The light is so bright that it hurts my eyes, but I don't want to turn it off because I need proof that this is actually happening. I don't know what to do with my hands, so I leave them at my sides, soaking with sweat. Kissing. Hand at the button on the front of my pants. This girl is out of my league—I know it, but she knows it too. She knows where this is going even when I don't have an idea. She climbs on top of me, her face inches away from mine, and closes her eyes. For whatever reason, I can't stop thinking about that show she was on, how she was just a kid like me back then, and how everything in her life transpired to bring her to this moment, to this bunk on this bus in the desert, with a loser kid like me inside her. It sort of makes me sad. Then she says something like "Cum in me" or "Cum on me," barely whispered over the noise of her panting, and I don't catch it. But I realize there is a pretty big difference between the two options.

I nod my head. I begin to realize that "hot" girls come with crazier flaws than the rest of us—the hotter they are, the crazier the flaws. Our knees touch. We shiver in the heat. Our skins stick together like leather in the summer. If only my friends could see me now. She pulls her dress back on and puts her number into my phone. We both know it's a meaningless gesture. Then she steps off the bus, back into her life. I fall asleep with a smile on my face. I am living the dream.

Months, miles, who's counting anymore? Only the events stand out. One night, I am inexplicably getting drunk at a motel in Daytona Beach (I think it was Daytona Beach), some morbid, Mid-Century Modern place called the Thunderbird Motel. I only remember the name because I still have the postcard I stole from the lobby. The parking lot faced the highway, the balconies faced out to the Atlantic. Landlocked tears versus limitless possibilities. I remember thinking that was *way* symbolic. I was pretty drunk at the time.

Girls were there, poor, wide-eyed things from tiny, hopeless towns, and they just stared at us, stood there biting their lips because they didn't know what to say or how to say it. You could tell their minds were blown. Maybe that was just the pot though. The Animal and I did our best to chat them up, but after a while, we just gave up. It wasn't worth the effort. So mostly we all just stood out there on the balcony, watched the moon ripple on the Atlantic, listened to the traffic on the other side of the building. No one was talking. The party was kind of dead.

Then, from inside the room, came a hideous crash. A scream. We ran back inside to see a kid—long hair, jean shorts, no shirt—lying flat on his back, blood pouring from his head. He was covered in white powder, and crushed ceiling tiles were scattered around him. We thought he was dead. But then he sat up, stared at us, and smiled. There were several gaps where some teeth should've been. Without saying a word, he got to his feet, walked into the kitchen, and came back with two tallboys of Natural Light. He drank one and offered the other to me. Dumbfounded, I took it from him.

"Hey, yer that guy, right?" he said, wobbling slightly.

I nodded.

"Oh, man, you fucking suck."

Everyone in the room was mortified. They were look-ing at the hole in the ceiling, the tiles on the floor, at everything except this bleeding maniac standing in the middle of the room. Nobody knew who he was, nobody knew where he came from. He was the first real person I'd met in almost a year. He had balls instead of brains, and you need people like that in your life because they keep you honest. I liked him immediately.

"Why are you bleeding?" I asked him.

"I tried to jump through the fuckin' ceiling but I missed."

It made sense. I liked him even more.

The sun is coming up now over the Atlantic, big and red, setting the sky on fire. We're standing on the balcony, the Animal and me, drinking tallboys. The crazy kid is out there with us too, still shirtless, the blood dried in midtrickle down his face. Pretty much everyone else had passed out, the girls curled up in chairs, eyes closed tight, mouths small and taut, peaceful, innocent, beautiful, the way all girls look when they're asleep. It was kind of magical, the air effervescent with ocean mist, the morning sky glowing like embers. Beneath us, the waves rush the beach, then quickly retreat with a soft hiss . . . God's white noise, the kind psychiatrists pay good money to fill their waiting rooms with. My old life seems so far away now. I'm stoned and happy. My eyelids are getting heavy. I'm not long for the world. Then, without being prompted, the kid starts talking.

"I wuz pretty much born in an abortion clinic," he says, waking the Animal and me from our trances. "I wuz born in Tampa in May of '82. They razed the hospital, and by January '83 it was an abortion clinic."

He's just staring out at the Atlantic, his face expressionless, and I can't help but laugh. Lines like that are showstoppers, and I definitely heard the record skip in my brain. Finally, I'm compelled to ask this crazy kid what his name is, and he tells me it's John. John Miller. It's sort of a letdown. He deserved a better name than that, something like Talon or Falcon or Buck, something befitting a wild-haired feral child, the kind that crawls out of the jungle once every fifty years. The kind of name suitable for a big-game tracker, or a roughneck on an oil derrick, or a drunken, dusty gunslinger. Instead, he got stuck with John Miller. It makes him sound like a chiropractor. His parents really fucked him over.

"Well, John Miller," I said, eyelids drooping like some cartoony drunk's, "your name fucking sucks."

"Yeah, I know it," John Miller winced, finishing his

umpteenth tallboy of the night (or morning). "My parents really fucked me over."

Great minds. Kismet. All that bullshit. I love this kid.

"I think we should hang out more," I told him, leaning on the railing of the balcony for support. "You should give me your e-mail address, and the next time we're in here we should hang."

"Yeah, definitely, I love doin' dumb shit," John Miller said, then staggered inside to get a pen or throw up or something. The Animal and I stare out at the quickly brightening beach. We should be going soon.

"That kid is great." I laugh.

"Eh, he's okay," the Animal snorts. He's a man of few words.

We go back to staring at the Atlantic. There's really nothing else to say. The sun clears the horizon, making the surface of the ocean shimmer like a tray of diamonds, and from the other side of the motel comes the sound of the first trucks of the day, downshifting on their way out of town. We should've been back on the bus by now. People are probably starting to worry.

Then there's another crash behind us, and we whirl around to see John Miller standing there, holding a sheet of paper in his hand. On it, he's scrawled his e-mail address: *Disaster69@aol.com*. It's strangely perfect.

"Nobody ever calls me John," he said, handing the sheet to me.

"Yeah, I can kind of see why." I laugh.

And then, the Animal and I are in the lobby of the motel, calling our tour manager from a courtesy telephone. He asks where we are and says he'll send a cab to get us. He hangs up in a huff. I think we woke him up. We sit out on the curb and watch the trucks rumble by, off to who knows where, back who knows when. You can feel the heat rising from the ground already. Finally, the cab comes to get us, one of those old bangers with the velvety interior that always smells like cigarettes, the kind they have in every city that's *not* New York, and we have the driver take us back to whatever the arena was called. I roll down my window, lean my head back on the velvet, and close my eyes. The last thing I see is the cabdriver checking me out in the rearview. He looks like the kind of guy they'd cast to play a Vietnam vet in some movie.

It's not important. Like I said, after a while, you don't remember the days, just the events. I'll remember this day because there were *two* of them. The first was meeting the Disaster. The second happened when I got back to the bus, climbed into my bunk (the good-luck one), and checked my e-mail before I passed out. Only one new message was in my in-box. Sent at 3:47 a.m. From Her. I stare at it as the bus engine purrs to life, as we slip out of (I think) Daytona Beach. I can feel my heart pounding, and I'm pretty sure I know why. I should probably just delete it, go on with my life, but I don't. The computer takes forever opening it, as if God or Steve Jobs were asking me, "You *sure* you really wanna do this?" But then, there they are: Her words, filling my screen, and there's no turning back. I make it as far as the first line before I feel my heart burst in my chest.

I miss you.

14

I'm drunk and I probably shouldn't be writing this. But I really miss you tonight. I know I'm not supposed to—everyone tells me that—but I have for a while now, and it's not going away. I tried calling you the other night, from a pay phone so you wouldn't recognize the number, but the call didn't go through. Maybe Ma Bell doesn't want us to be together. Maybe God doesn't either. But I do. My life has come off track without you. I hardly know myself anymore. I need you.

I'm sorry about the past. I know I should've supported you; I was just scared of losing you. I didn't want to share you with everyone else. I was being selfish and I know that's what drove us apart. I forgive you for what you did. I would've probably done the same thing. I don't even care about it, to be honest. I just know that I need you back in my life, in any way possible, because it's getting harder and harder to get out of bed in the morning. It's scaring me.

Please write back.

I lie in my bunk, just reading the last line over and over. It's brutal. Beautiful. The saddest sentence I've ever seen. Three little words; so much weight, so much desperation alive within them. They're either the beginning, or the end, or both. Probably both. Rain pelts the window of the bus. Big, angry drops. Drops with a *purpose*. I watch the flat expanses of Florida blow by in a blur, nothing but swamps and palm trees and alligators. Things get less exotic the farther north you head: gated neighborhoods that back up to the interstate. Shopping malls on the horizon. Billboards for Jesus. The sky is low and pregnant and gray. The rain makes it even more depressing. I am stalling now.

I go back to that last line. *Please write back.* It paralyzes me. I close my eyes tightly, pull my blanket over my head, like a frightened kid trying to wish away the monster under his bed. I figure it's worth a shot. Sometimes I am willing to believe in anything if it means ignoring the reality of a situation. I open my eyes. *Please write back.* Fuck. I wish I had just deleted Her message. None of this would be happening if I did. I'd probably be asleep right now, dreaming of that fiery sunrise and that shimmering Atlantic. Instead I'm lying here, disarmed. Impotent. My head feels like I can't sit or lean on anything on the inside because it's all been freshly painted. Grays and pinks. And open some windows 'cause the air just isn't circulating the way it should. I realize I am stalling again. Fuck off.

She's always been succinct, but this line is Her masterwork. *Please write back.* It's funny because, according to my shrink, this is exactly what I've always wanted, what I've moaned and wailed and bled for my entire life: complete and total control. The past, the present, the future, it's all mine. I can erase history. I can eliminate what might be.

I can either write Her back, or not. It's that simple. Only it doesn't feel that way. It feels *profound,* frighteningly, cripplingly so. This is a fork in the road. A *Choose Your Own Adventure* book. A catastrophe waiting just around the corner. For the first time, it's *all up to me.* I realize in this instant that perhaps control isn't all it's cracked up to be. There's a reason I've never been able to grab the reins: I'm not strong enough to do it.

So now, not only am I paralyzed, but I'm furious at myself. I am useless. Weak. A boy in over his head, hiding behind tattoos and one-night stands. Trying hard to make sure nobody notices that he's drowning. The rain really gets angry now, hammering the roof of the bus like machine-gun fire. Heavy bullets from heaven. Heavy thoughts in my head. Do I really miss Her? Did I ever love Her? Can I hurt Her again? I've been staring at Her e-mail for more than an hour, and my computer is running on fumes. Just a tiny red sliver remains in the battery icon. I wish humans came with the same kind of indicator . . . it would make things much easier. You would know how to deal with every person on the planet, and I'd always be in the red. *Please write back.* The computer is dying. The rain is pushing the bus off the road. There's a twister coming. Make a decision. It's only a goddamn fucking e-mail. It's only my goddamn fucking life.

Good morning, I write to Her. *It's a new day.*

I press SEND, launch my reply out into the ether. I cannot control what happens next. If it finds Her, it was meant to be. Cosmic chance, divine fate, karma chameleon. Whatever you want to call it. After a few moments, my heart stops pounding and a strange calm fills my body. I am such a smug bastard that I think I've learned some sort of deep lesson from all this. I get out of my bunk and walk to the front lounge of the bus, feeling good about myself. A placid, Buddha-like smile slides across my face. I am enlightenment. I am Zen. I am not only the vase, I'm the space around the vase, and the space *within* the vase. You know, all that really deep stuff. I sit in the lounge and watch the towering storm clouds shower the flatlands and strip malls of Florida. Everyone else is asleep. I probably shouldn't be feeling good about myself. It was only a god-damn fucking e-mail.

15

It's a few weeks later. She's started sending me love letters now. Love e-mails, perfumed and pink, coquettish. Always in lowercase. You know what I mean. The first one caught me off guard . . . it was just a normal e-mail about some dream she had, about how she was standing on this cliff, overlooking the great expanses of the West, and below Her, on *another* cliff, a guy in a rhinestone suit, a game-show host, was tossing elephants up to Her, and she had to try to catch them on the head of a pin while a studio audience watched intently—that was the point of the game show—and how the elephants would drop out of the sky like great, bouncy balloons, and she'd try to balance them on the pin, only she couldn't do it, and they'd tumble down into a canyon and explode on the rocks below, in bright bursts of reds and blues, like cans of paint dropped off the roof of a building. Each time she'd let an elephant fall off the pin, the audience would boo a little louder, would hiss and inch a step closer to Her, until she was at the very edge of the cliff, looking down into the canyon, at the husks of elephants and the great, spattered rocks, and the game-show host would smile hideously, would pull a lever, and more elephants would start falling from the heavens, and the audience would lash out at Her, would tear Her clothing off and try to force Her onto the rocks, and how, just as the elephants began to rain down on Her, at the very moment Her heels were tipping back over the edge, Her roommate shook Her awake because she had been crying in Her sleep. Apparently, she had been having this dream ever since she was a child, though I'd never heard Her mention it before. Anyway, that's what she was going on about, and I was reading along halfheartedly, my eyes skimming over the endless sea of lowercase letters and parentheses (she loved parentheses), until, at the very end, they got snagged on three words, *i love you,* which she had planted at the very end of the e-mail, like a strategically placed bit of C-4, packed on just out of sight, waiting to detonate.

Of course, I caught it. I saw what she was up to. We terrorists know all the tricks of the trade. The problem was, I didn't do anything about it. I should've defused the bomb right then and there, should've cut the wires and tamped out the fuse, but I didn't . . . maybe because I felt sorry for Her, for the way I had treated Her, for the way Her life had come off track. Or maybe I still loved Her too. Either way, I let the *i love you* go unchecked, and that emboldened Her. A day later, she wrote another e-mail, used *i love you* twice, and after that, it was too late. There was no turning back. The messages have started to come with alarming frequency now—sometimes two or three a day—and I can do nothing to stop them. For a few days, I tried ignoring Her, but that just leads to even *more* e-mails . . . panicked, frightened ones, sent at four in the morning, full of spelling errors and run-on sentences and lines like *im sorry for being crazy*. You know what I mean. I am beginning to worry about Her. She is hardly sleeping, she is never going to class, she is fixating on me and slowly coming unraveled. I am beginning to think this was a terrible idea.

I don't know what caused all this. Actually, that's a lie; I do, I just don't want to admit it. Like everything else in my life, this was all my fault. See, one night last week, in a moment of weakness after the after-party, when the moon hung low and bright over a stretch of I-95 somewhere in southeast Georgia, when I was awake on the bus and sad and really, really drunk, I *may* have written that I was falling in love with Her again. It was probably a mistake. I didn't even mean it—I don't even remember *writing* it—but she didn't know that, and by the time I woke up the following afternoon, she had replied with three separate e-mails, each sent a few hours apart, and each crazier than the last. I rolled over in my bunk and went back to sleep. I am an addict. I am an idiot. My sickness is severe.

The worst thing about Her e-mails isn't even the *i love you*s. Don't get me wrong, those are pretty bad, but what's even worse is that when I read them, it's almost as if I'm looking at myself. She's started writing like me now, all lowercase and parenthetical, full of tangents and angles, half-realized thoughts thrown into go-nowhere paragraphs. She has become narcissistic and maniacal, obsessive and pathological, only she hides it all beneath a thin layer of self-effacement. I've been getting by on this same trick for years, and I'm beginning to realize that I can be insufferable because of it. With each e-mail I read, I wondered more and more why no one has ever bothered to tell me this. Or hauled off and belted me in the face. Anyone besides the philosopher, that is, but he had just cause. I wouldn't want to spend a minute with me, that's for certain.

We're somewhere in South Carolina now, in some awful strip club off the interstate. The kind of place where they serve breakfast and the parking lot is loaded with truckers looking for a quickie. We came here as a joke, and I'm the only one who isn't listening. Instead, I'm on my Drone, reading another of Her endless e-mails. In front of me, a too skinny girl with bad makeup and dead eyes asks me if I want a dance. I say yes, then instantly regret it. Under the black light in a strip club, everything takes the shape of regret sooner or later.

She puts out her cigarette (she has a pack of Camels stuffed into her thigh-highs) and goes to work. I'm trying to write Her back, but there are breasts in my light. "I'm only doing this to pay my way through school," the dancer says to me, and I think to myself, somewhere, there is a university full of strippers paying their way through. Somewhere out there, a college takes tuition payments in dollar bills. I look in her dead eyes and lie, "You're too pretty for this. You should model." She smiles and I can see the stains on her teeth, all blotchy and off-white beneath the black light. I wish she'd stop. She asks me what I'm writing, and I lie again, tell her I'm writing a letter to my wife. I ask her to press SEND and she obliges.

"You're too young to be married," she whispers through her hideous teeth.

"She's my second wife," I say. "My first wife died in a fire. My whole house burned down, and she was in there with my kids. They're all dead."

She pauses on my lap, midgrind. You have to say something pretty fucked-up to get a stripper to do something like that. I am on a roll now, and I don't want to stop. I tell her that I was just e-mailing my second wife to tell her it's over, that I want a divorce. I've told my wife she doesn't understand my needs, that we grew apart long ago. I've told her I'm in love with another woman. As long as a guy has a sob story, he doesn't have to throw out dollar bills. If I string together every single heartbreaking story I have, they would measure out to an entire *night* of free lap dances. The stripper stares at me, then continues grinding, occasionally shooting the bouncer across the room a panicked glance. I think she mouths *Help* to him, but I can't be sure. She probably thinks I'm a serial killer or something. I love it. There is a special place in hell for people like me.

The dance ends and she doesn't even ask if I'd like a second. She just gathers up her underwear and makes a beeline for the bar. As she walks away, she reaches into her stocking and pulls out another Camel. I have fantasies of my e-mail making it back to Her with faint traces of smoke and Victoria's Secret Vanilla body spray on it. I imagine Her opening it and pausing as a few bits of glitter fall out of the subject line. That would certainly make everything easier. I laugh to myself and take another pull off my bottle of Bud. I am drunk in a strip club in South Carolina. I finish my drink and walk back to the bus.

Two days later, we're in Somewhere, North Carolina. The tour is wrapping up, just a quick run up the East Coast and a left at I-80 in New Jersey is all that stands between me and Chicago. I don't want to go back there, and not just because it means I'll have to deal with Her. I have no place to live, either, and even though I swore I'd never go back to my parents' house, it's looking more and more like that'll be the case. It's pathetic. Midway through the tour, the Animal and I had made vague plans to get a place together, but who knows if he even remembers. I'm too embarrassed to ask him anyway.

So I'm lying awake one morning, looking out my window at some dreary North Carolina parking lot, dreading my future, when all of a sudden there's a tremendous pounding on the door of our bus. At first, I think I'm hearing things, but the pounding just gets louder—WHUMP! WHUMP! WHUMP WHUMP WHUMP!—like some ham-fisted maniac trying to bash his way onto the bus. I don't get up, but from my bunk I can hear our road manager swing the door open, ask someone what the fuck he wants, then there's about a minute of silence. I hear our road manager get off the bus, and then some shouting. Someone is asking if I'm on the bus. I'm sitting up in my bunk now, ears straining for the slightest sound, and I hear a pair of footsteps getting back on board.

They walk the length of the bus, come to a stop outside my bunk, and our road manager pulls back the curtain. Standing there, next to him, soaking wet, shirtless, and wearing a long pair of cutoff jean shorts, is John Miller. The Disaster. I blink at him, he cracks a stupid smile at me.

"*This* came for you," our road manager deadpans, then walks back to the front of the bus.

I get out of my bunk and just sort of stand there, in my underwear, next to John Miller. He's carrying a black garbage bag, which, I assume, holds his worldly possessions. His lower lip bulges out from his face, a thick wad of Skoal peeking out slightly. A mesh trucker's cap—not the Hollywood douche-bag kind, but an actual cap, made for actual truckers, purchased at an actual truck stop—sits in a peak atop his greasy head. Water drips down his forehead, leaving streak marks. He is tanned and bird-chested, skinny everywhere except his stomach, which protrudes out comically, proudly, a testament to the many tallboys he's conquered in his time. He looks as if he just stepped off the cover of Lynyrd Skynyrd's *Street Survivors* album, or maybe like a slightly soaked Allman Brother. He is a damp redneck ghost, a Southern-rock relic. And he's dripping on my bare feet.

"What are you *doing* here?" I ask, pulling on a pair of jeans.

"I never heard from you, so I figgered I'd just stop by," he drawls. He seems distinctively more *Confederate* since I saw him last, like he'd just discovered his inner Stonewall Jackson. "Ahm hungry, you wanna go eat or som'thin'?"

I don't know what to say, and I especially don't want to know how he got so wet, so I just sort of nod my head. John Miller drops his garbage bag on the floor, between the rows of bunks, and clomps off to the front of the bus. I grab a T-shirt and follow him, not knowing where we're going or how we're getting there. We step off the bus, into the damp North Carolina morning, and trudge across the parking lot. The club where we'll play tonight leans off in the distance, empty kegs of beer stacked in a pyramid by the back door. John Miller eyes them hungrily. He is still not wearing a shirt. I watch the muscles in his shoulders move back and forth beneath his shoulder blades, which are so sharp they could be weapons. His body (save for his beer gut) is sinewy and taut, stringy yet firm, in that weird and decidedly *Southern* way, the way that all goes to hell when you hit thirty. He's never lifted a weight in his life, and someday it will catch up with him.

We walk alongside a two-lane road, our hands in our pockets, and John Miller tells me his life story. His parents run a mortuary in Jacksonville, Florida, and they want him to be more like his older brothers, who are both licensed by the state Division of Funeral, Cemetery and Consumer Services. He went to community college to get a degree in mortuary science, but dropped out because, as he put it, "morticians don't get laid." He has been arrested "a couple of times." He is "a fucking massive" Jacksonville Jaguars fan, the first I've ever met. And, more than anything else in the world, he claims to be one of two people in Florida who know the actual burial spot of Ronnie Van Zant.

So, after meeting me in Daytona Beach a few weeks back, he decided that I was his best bet out of Jacksonville. He went online, found out where we'd be playing, and, using the little bit of money he had saved up, bought a one-way ticket to Raleigh. He doesn't say how he got from the airport to the front door of our tour bus, and I don't ask. I was too busy trying to figure out how he got on an airplane if he wasn't wearing a shirt.

A light mist is falling now, flecks of rain dancing in the gray morning air. We walk past a retention pond, surrounded by a rusty chain-link fence. The grass is knee-high, swaying like fields of thin cornstalks. The sidewalk was long ago overtaken by weeds, and bright yellow flowers poke through cracks in the concrete. No one has cared about this stretch of land for some time now. Decades maybe. Bodies are probably hiding in the grass. Or alligators. There is no one for miles. No cars, no noise, no humanity. John Miller and I are the last two people on earth.

Eventually, we make our way to a stretch of highway dotted with low-lying strip malls. Nail salons. A scary bar called the Grizzly. A pet store. It's depressing. Cars plod by, weighed down by life. Eventually, we come across a diner, one of those sock-hop fifties-type places where everything is covered in chrome and checkered tile. We go inside and have a seat. A bubbly jukebox is in the corner, with murals of Elvis and James Dean painted on the walls. A neon GOOD EATS sign behind the register. A castrated motorcycle leaning by the bathroom. Authentic 45s dangling from the ceiling. You've probably been here. You know what I'm talking about.

The place is packed with churchgoers refueling after a long morning spent repenting and praising. Old women with hair as white as snow glance up from their menus, plastic-framed glasses teetering on the brinks of their noses. Ruddy-cheeked kids with syrup on their church clothes cower behind their parents. Not exactly our crowd. A plump waitress shuffles over to our booth, looks right at John Miller, and tells him that he needs to be wearing a shirt in here. She calls him "sir" in that con-descending way only those who wield temporary author-ity can, all slowlike, with the *i* drawn out for emphasis: "siiiir." Bank tellers are especially good at this. Flight at-tendants too.

Anyway, John Miller doesn't have any money, so I buy him a T-shirt from the gift shop. I make sure to buy him the biggest one available, and in North Carolina, they make them plenty big. I return to the booth with a Hanes Beefy-T, XXXL. An illustration of a waitress on roller skates is on the front. John Miller doesn't even blink while he pulls it over his head. He sits there, drinking his coffee, his actual trucker's cap turned backward, wearing a giant tent for a shirt. None of this bothers him in the least. He is unflappable. On the wall behind his head is a metal Route 66 road sign, and a framed photo of a shiny '57 Chevy. The caption reads AN AMERICAN CLASSIC. Ex-actly.

John Miller and I settle into the booth. I'm not even hungry, but I find myself looking through the menu, eye-ing the All-Day Breakfast selections and the Home-Style Dinners. They have hamburgers called The Marilyn and

The Big Bopper, tributes to icons who died of a mysterious drug overdose and a plane crash in Iowa, respectively. This does not make me as sad as you would think. Someday everyone will die. Not everyone will get a sandwich named after him or her.

I look up from the menu and see that John Miller is staring at me, with a rabid, faraway look in his eyes. A Southern look, honed by peering off into great distances, searching for clues on the horizon. We don't have that look in Chicago. He asks what I was laughing about, and I tell him the joke I just made to myself about the hamburgers. He doesn't get it. Why would he? He is a maniac, he is just embarking on an adventure; he has no time to think about death. The waitress shuffles back to take our orders. John Miller is having some ghastly thing with eggs and bacon and french fries. I tell the waitress I want the repression burger, fifties style. She doesn't laugh, doesn't even bat an eyelash; instead, she sighs and tells me it's too early to order anything off the dinner menu. It was a pretty dumb joke. I order an omelet instead.

"So whudyou guys do for *fun?*" John Miller asks me, eyes wide now.

"I don't know, man. To be honest, we don't have a lot of fun," I say. "Basically we just drive from one place to the next. We play shows. . . . I don't know. It's not fun, man. Not after a while."

He chuckles. "You awghta come down to Jacksonville with me sometime. If you think *this* ain't fun, you ain't seen nothin'. Man, all we got down there is the fuckin' *water.*"

I smile. Suddenly, I care about John Miller more than anyone else on the planet. He is a believer. He sees the good in everything. He is unscathed by life, not because he hasn't lived, but because he hasn't slowed down long enough to notice that he's bleeding. He is free, like the hoboes of Kerouac. If he wanted to, John Miller could disappear right now, could pick up his garbage bag, toss it over his shoulder, and vanish into thin air. No one would ever come looking for him, and he wouldn't expect them to. John Miller is unencumbered, he carries no baggage, has no phobias or neuroses. He asks no big questions, does not worry about what tomorrow may bring, because he lives only in the *now*. He is unlike anyone I have ever known before. I want him to teach me *everything,* how to embalm a body or hop a train, how to go through life free of burden and fear, how to be truly, maddeningly, dazzlingly happy. I want more than anything for him to like me. So I tell him the story of the actress I slept with in Las Vegas, about how she climbed in my bunk and told me to cum inside her, about how I haven't called her since and probably never will again. He laughs and pounds the table with his fists and shouts stuff like "No shit!" and "God-*damn!*" at the top of his lungs, making the old, churchgoing crows stare at us over their plastic-framed glasses. I tell him about my *other* conquests too . . . the pretty tattoo artist in Phoenix, the girl with the studded tongue in St. Louis, the Chilean girl in Milwaukee who said her dad was Tom Araya from Slayer . . . and now John Miller is practically rolling on the floor, guffawing and repeatedly spitting out "Je-zus *Christ!*" with such fervor that the manager has to come over and remind us that this is a family restaurant. We ignore him and just keep right on shouting, cursing, being terrible. Offending churchly old women and meek, stammering managers. I feel alive for the first time in months.

But then, as our waitress tosses our food in front of us with a huff, I find that there's no second act. I've confessed *all* of my sins to John Miller, every dirty deed I've done since we hit the road, and now as he stares at me expectantly, over a steaming plate of eggs and bacon and fries, I find I've got nothing left to tell him. There's a deflating moment of silence. My omelet quivers slightly on my fork. John Miller wipes the tears from his eyes and exhales deeply.

"Shiiiit" is all he says.

We eat our meals quietly, much to the relief of the skinny manager, who still watches us suspiciously from the cash register. The tiny jukebox on our table makes me think about the first night I met Her . . . that time in Chicago so many years ago, back when we were young and unafraid, sort of like John Miller. How we kissed on the street, held hands beneath the table. How I traced the small of Her back with my fingers. And, oh, how much distance we've covered since then, how much we've changed, two arrows shot in opposite directions. She's still writing me love letters and I am unmoved by them. They're just words. I realize I do not love Her. I wish I hadn't told Her I did.

I drop a quarter in the jukebox, summon the ghosts of ducktailed rockabilly cats and tousled-haired teen idols, sweet-voiced doo-wop singers and yelping young Negroes with wild pompadours. They were the kings of their era, the Imperials and the Belmonts, the Diamonds and the Del-Vikings. They were the savages of the decade, pounding the piano, and thumping the upright bass. Pulling pints of whiskey from their back pockets. Groping girls. Having wild times. None of that mattered in the end; they're all dead now. Time always wins. Suddenly, I can't bear to look at their names. One time, when I was a kid, my dad took me and my brother to a diner like this, with the same jukeboxes on the tables, and he let us each play a song. He gave us quarters and helped us scroll through the selections. My brother chose Buckner and Garcia's "Pac-Man Fever." I don't know why I remember that.

This place has a sadness, an indefinable, intangible dread. John Miller doesn't notice. He's too busy shoveling food into his mouth. Watching him eat is disgusting, just a blur of elbows and french fries. Belching. He never comes up for air. I stare at him with a mixture of admiration and disdain. I get the feeling most people look at him this way. He doesn't notice that either.

"Whas the matter?" he asks, his mouth full of yolk and potatoes. "You not hungry?"

I shrug.

"I gonna tell you something, man, based on my observations, and I hope you don't git too mad or take it th' wrawng way." He reaches in his back pocket for his can of Skoal. "You promise me you won't take it th' wrawng way now, right?"

I nod.

"See, th' thing with you is, man, you jess seem so sad. Like, sadder than prolly anyone I ever met. An' from what I heard, you ain't got nothing to be sad about. Now I may not have th' whole pitchure, and I may not know you all that well, but based on what I've observed, on watchin' you look around th' place, not eatin', lissenin' to you talk about all those pretty girls you been with . . . you jess seem *sad,* man. It's in yer eyes. Shit, but if I'm wrawng, jess tell me. Don't git upset."

He is not wrawng. I begin to worry that he can see right through me, that he can tell I'm a gigantic phony, perhaps the phoniest person alive. So I tell him the story of Her, the whole story, from when we met to that time I left Her crying on the bedroom floor, picking up pieces of Her shattered cell phone. That time when I was so unbelievably cruel. I tell him how she used to make me feel, how I opened myself up to Her and how she let me down more than anyone else has ever let another human being down. I tell him about the brawl with the philosopher and the trip to the emergency room. And finally, I tell him about the love letters she's been sending me, and how *they* make me feel . . . like I'm snared, being pulled back down again. The waitress comes and clears our plates away, and I keep talking. She returns to refill our coffees, and I'm still talking. I talk and talk, until there's nothing left to say, until I'm trailing off, ending sentences with "and you know . . ." and eyes into the distance. When I'm finished, John Miller is the only person alive who knows the *entire* story of Her and me. I've told it to no one else. I'm not sure why.

We sit there for a heavy minute, John Miller preparing his Skoal. He holds the can between his thumb and middle finger, flicks his wrist, thumps the can with his pointer finger, packing the tobacco in one fluid, blurry motion. He tilts the can toward me, nods his head, but I say no. Then he takes a massive wad and crams it into his bottom lip. It bulges just like his stomach. We sit there for another heavy minute, and I'm wondering if he was even listening to me. He spits into his coffee cup, leans *waaaay* back in the booth, eyes me with that country-mile stare, and finally, regally, speaks.

"Lissen, man. I'm gonna say it again. I may not know you all that well, but I understand whatcher goin' through," he drawls. "I been through it, my brothers' been through it, everybody's been through it. We all got a crisis, an' somehow, there's always a girl involved in the creation. There was this girl back in Jacksonville that I loved. Shit, I was gonna marry her. We didn't have a care in the world, not one. An' then one day, she finds out she's pregnant. We're gonna have a baby, an' I jess lose it. I don't know what happened. I wasn't ready. I was terrified. So I left."

He gets quiet, spits in his coffee cup. Someone plays a song on the jukebox in the corner. I wish they hadn't.

"I left her an' then she didn't have the baby. She loss it, you know? Pretty early on, but long enough, y'know? The doctors said there was nothin' she coulda done different. But I knew she loss that baby because of me. Because I left. She knew it too. We broke up an' I haven't talked to her since. This was jess about a year ago now, an' since then I dropped out of school an' got arrested a coupla times, because I was so mad at myself. I still am. I think about that baby all the time, and how it's dead on account of me. Woulda been a boy. . . .

"So I been runnin' ever since. I can't run from me though. An' that's my crisis. I know I got to deal with it, I jess don't know if I ever will." He smiles slightly. "What you got is a crisis of confidence. With that girl, with yourself. An' you gotta deal with it. Now, I jess met you and I don't know how you do it, but you gotta. Or else it'll eat you up an' you'll end up like me, with nothin' and no place to go."

John Miller spits again into his coffee cup. The manager thinks about saying something from behind the register, but he decides differently. The ghost of Fats Domino wafts along in the air like a sad, black balloon. There's nothing left to say. We pay our check and walk back into the drizzly North Carolina rain. John Miller doesn't talk much on the walk back, and I get the feeling that he's never told anyone else about his crisis. By the time we get to the bus, our clothes are soaked. John Miller hasn't had a dry minute since he got here. That night, after we're done with our last song, I tell the audience that I love them. I don't know why I did it. From the side of the stage, in a rumpled white T-shirt with a roller-skating waitress on the front, John Miller, Southern Sage, is smiling. Chicago looms large on the horizon, just weeks away now. For the first time in forever, its jagged, gray skyline doesn't seem all that ominous.

16

John Miller is my new roommate. Right now, he and I are sharing twin beds in my old bedroom, but we're moving out soon. When I showed up at my parents' house with him in tow, my mom's jaw about hit the floor. He had managed to make himself look extrapathetic by not showering for a week, so his hair stuck out in all directions from underneath his trucker's cap. I told my mom that he had no other place to go, that taking him in was an act of charity. It was an easy sell; my mom loves charity. She emptied his garbage bag into the washing machine, made him some food, sat back, and watched the elbows fly. Nobody eats like John Miller. It's like being in shop class or something. Debris everywhere. You should be required to wear safety glasses whenever he's at the table.

My mom loved him immediately, leaned against the refrigerator with arms crossed, listened to his stories about Jacksonville and his two older brothers with glee. She watched him saw through meals and thought he was just the greatest—a real character from the Deep South, right here in her tastefully wallpapered kitchen. John Miller was laying it on thick too, complimenting her cooking with an antebellum grace ("This here cake is better than my grandmama's") and offering to work on the hydrangeas out back ("There was a time when me and my two brothers had ourselves a lan'scapin' business"). He seemed to get more Southern as the situation demanded it, and right now he was talking like some combination of Foghorn Leghorn and Roscoe P. Coltrane. I half expected him to pull a coonhound out of his pocket. It was amazing to watch him work. There was an art to it. His eyes were constantly darting around the room, sizing everything—and everyone—up, sussing out their weaknesses, plying them with praise. John Miller was a natural-born con man, a used-car salesman, a lawyer's lawyer. Naturally, my dad didn't like him, but I could not care less; in a few days, we'd be set up in our own place, and then the real fun would begin.

In the midst of all this, I wasn't even thinking of Her, and I didn't until later that night, when John Miller was buzz-sawing through sleep (he did everything abrasively). I lay there in my old bed, thinking of the times she had laid next to me, the summer nights when my parents went away to their place in New Buffalo, on the shore of Lake Michigan, and she and I would sleep wrapped around each other, the window open, the cool air kissing our shoulders. I had long ago decided that I didn't love Her anymore, but on certain nights, when I lay awake while everyone else slept, eyes wide-open in the dark, I knew that was a lie, or at least I was pretty sure it was.

Maybe I *did* love Her, more than I'd ever loved anyone or anything else in my life. Perhaps I had spent the past six months trying to convince myself otherwise, blaming Her for things that were not Her fault, getting drunk and screwing around with women who weren't Her and never could be. John Miller, wise son of the St. John's, he knew this the minute I started rattling off my sexual conquests in that North Carolina diner, could see right through my bravado, my act. He knew I was lying, that all of it was a show and that deep down I ached for Her, even if he didn't know who *Her* was just yet. Which is why he took pity on me, laid that sob story on me . . . he wanted me to know that it was *okay* to be in love with Her, that it was probably inevitable, and that, if I ever wanted to fix my— as he put it—"crisis of confidence" and be happy and not live out of a garbage bag, well, then there was probably no better place to start than with Her. Either that or he was trying to con me. I haven't decided.

But now, as I lie here in the night watching the moon-light pour in through my bedroom window, my mind wandering back to those sweet summer nights when our feet would touch at the bottom of my twin-size bed, I am at least willing to consider that I loved Her. Perhaps even admit it. Almost by accident, I think of Her face, slender and pale, and those big, beautiful eyes that, on nights like this, caught moonbeams and held them quivering and soft on her lashes, and I know that it's all over for me. I can hear my pulse quicken against my pillow, can physically *feel* my heart roll over in my chest. Our brains may lie to us, but our hearts never do. . . . I could deny it to myself all I wanted, but I loved Her. I needed Her. And she needed to know that I did. In that instant, I could tell where this night was heading; we insomniacs know when sleep's not in the cards.

In that instant, a desperation had come over me; a panic. I didn't know what to do but I knew I had to do it *now,* so I sat up in my bed, ran my fingers through my hair, and decided to do something irrational. And now I am hopping around in the dark, pulling my jeans on, trying not to make a sound or break my neck. John Miller is snoring *biblically* at this point, as if he's got locusts in his throat, and as I slip out of the bedroom, he sputters and snorts, comes close to surfacing, but doesn't wake up. If he did, I would've smothered him with a pillow. Such is my mania.

Before I know it, I am sitting in my brother's car, trying to figure out how to make the garage door open without waking them up. Did you know that with enough force you can make even a mechanical garage door open? Neither did I, until I found myself squatting and sweating, working my fingers under the lip of the thing, then gritting my teeth and *lifting.* I grunt and swear under my breath, nearly kill myself, and have to rest the door on my shoulder. But, eventually, I get it up, push it over my head, and it didn't make a sound as it swung open. I step out into the driveway, pale blue in the moonlight, and look up at my parents' bedroom window to make sure they're still sleeping. I'm not really sure why I'm doing any of this . . . I am twenty-five years old, I can come and go as I please. But something about tonight lends

itself to secrecy. I start the car as quietly as I can, winc-
ing as the engine wakes from its sleep. It hasn't moved
since my brother went away to college, and it takes a
few seconds to shake the cobwebs. Then I drive out and
onto the street, slowly, no headlights on, and I'm off. At
the very least, I know now I can break into my parents'
garage if the situation warrants it.

The streets of the North Shore are deserted, dead. The
neat brick houses are sleeping, their shutters closed tight.
Even the lampposts have dozed off. I drive around for a
bit, past Avoca Park, where I used to play Youth Soccer,
down to the Baha'i temple, its dome illuminated for no
one in particular. I don't know where I'm going, so I just
keep driving, my bones buzzing and my head fuzzy, that
kind of feeling you only get when you're awake while the
rest of the world is asleep. An uninterrupted stream of
classic rock is on the radio, the DJs playing long songs like
"Layla" so they can go for smoke breaks. I am driving with
the windows down, and the night feels damp on my face.
I'm the only one breathing it in right now, the only one
alive. I glance down at the clock on the dashboard. Jesus,
it's three thirty in the morning. It's Monday now. Off in
the distance, I see a truck stopping at each house, tossing
newspapers out of the passenger door. I throw the car in
park and turn the radio down, listen to hear the thump of
the Monday edition landing on each driveway. It's a sound
most people don't ever get to hear, but if you've heard
it once—if you've been wandering the streets while the
businessmen sleep—then you never forget it.

I decide to drive into the city. Maybe I will call Her

and wake Her up. I reach into my pocket and realize I've
left my cell phone sitting next to my bed. Oh, well. It
will have to be a surprise then. I don't know what time
she wakes up for class, or even if she *has* class, but I'm
pretty sure it's not going to be for a few hours now.
I've got time to kill and nowhere to kill it. I steer the
car back toward Sheridan, take it over the harbor, pass
the Baha'i again, its dome still lit. I follow the road as
it twists through the campus of Northwestern, all sand-
stone monuments to higher learning, through Centennial
Park, with Lake Michigan in the distance, inky black and
refracting the moon into a million shards that dance on
its choppy waves. There are lights even farther off, ships
maybe, blinking red and white. I wonder if she's awake
right now? I wonder if I should try to call Her from a pay
phone?

Sheridan presses on, past Kedzie, which isn't the
Kedzie where the philosopher and I brawled, but close
enough, cuts around the cemetery, so big and full of
ghosts right now, dives through the campus of Loyola, red
bricks and Jesuit priests, and finally tosses me into the
mouth of Lake Shore, that great road hugging the banks of
the lake, the site of many an existential episode. Cars are
on the opposite side of the road now, and their headlights
make me jump. For a while there, I had sort of forgotten about the possibilities of other people because my
pulse was hopping and I was thinking of Her and reveling
in the solitude of the night. I wonder where these other
people are going, and who's waiting for them when they
get there? Maybe no one. I think of John Miller and his

garbage bag full of clothes and heart full of crisis. I think of his dead son. I press on and Lake Shore unwinds in front of me, the great lights and buildings of Chicago appearing through the passenger window of the car.

I turn off at Roscoe, cross over Broadway, and suddenly I am parking the car on Clark. Up ahead, the lights of the diner shine forlornly onto the empty streets. I'm drawn to them like a moth. It seems like I always end up here, in this diner, in this booth, and it's always night. I haven't been back downtown since the night of our record-release party, when I got drunk and went home with that girl who shouted all those *Oh, God*s and wrote *Bastard* on my hand. I wonder if anyone ever told Her about that. I wonder if she cared. The diner is practically vacant right now, at what I'm guessing is around 5:00 or 6:00 a.m. (I don't own a watch). A few loners seated at the counter. A cute lesbian couple cuddled together by the window. A cook with tattoos on his forearms. A waitress who looks like a purple-haired librarian. Me. The lights make it feel yellow in here, the way all-night diners always feel when they're empty and the morning skies are still dark. Or maybe that's just me; my eyes never adjust to the light.

I order a coffee from the librarian. Ask her what time it is. She tells me it's four forty-five. Fuck. We used to kill hours here, splitting coffees, cracking jokes. We had no place to go, and we were in no hurry to get there. Things are different now. I'm older and impatient. It's because of the road, of the lost hours spent wandering the streets of strange cities after sound check, or slumped in a chair backstage, killing time before the show, listening to the kids shout on the other side of the wall. There are only two constants on the road: waiting around, and the knowledge that you'll be doing it again tomorrow, only in a different city. It *kills* you eventually. Now, I hate waiting for anything. But at this moment, I've got no other choice.

I drink my coffee slowly. Stare at the lesbians in the window. Occasionally, they notice, and I avert my eyes, pretend I'm studying the menu intently. My brain is still trying to convince me that I don't love Her, replaying a million conversations about Freud and the unconscious self, conversations I entertained only out of politeness but never made an attempt to comprehend. My brain shows me highlights of our greatest hits, the fights, the tears, the doubts. It unspools footage from the future, of our place in Berkeley, of the two bookish kids we will raise, of the co-op market on the corner. I am fat and unhappy, prone to gazing out the window, thinking about what could have been. I have glasses and am wearing a sweater. Have gone soft. It is boho-intellectual-postmodern-think-globally-act-locally-organic-produce-petition-signing-expensive-coffee-drinking hell. I shudder a bit. Call the librarian over and order breakfast.

Someone once told me that digging up the past has two sides: The pro is that you remember things you had forgotten about. Unfortunately, the con is the exact same thing. That may scare some people away, might force them to always be moving forward, never looking back, not for a second. But not me. I'm a believer. In my heart, I know that nothing is ever finished. I can't close the door on anything. Right now, I need to follow my heart; I need to have a little faith. So, against my brain's advice, I wolf down some eggs, slurp up my coffee, and leave the diner with a newfound sense of purpose. A mission. I walk Clark with a full head of steam, burning seconds with each step. But then I realize that it's still too early to accomplish much of anything, so I go back to my brother's car, fall asleep in the backseat. I awake to somber, light purple skies and the sound of early rising commuters. For a second, I think about what my parents will think when they discover John Miller and one empty twin-size in my bedroom. Then I think about John Miller, and what *he'll* do when my parents find him there. But only for a second. Then I'm off to Her place.

I cut through Cabrini, hoping to avoid the early morning traffic. I'm not actually sure why . . . it's barely 6:00 a.m., and I'm in no hurry to get to Her apartment. The city is beautiful now, the Near North Side still slumbering in its affluence, the coffee shops and charcuteries still shuttered tight. I'm watching Chicago awaken. A ghost with no real place to go. But I'm getting antsy, so enough of the ethereal shit. I drive to Her building, slanted and slightly crumbling, the kind of decay rich people pay good money for. I park the car and sit for a few minutes, studying Her window for any sign of life. The same curtains are starting to glow in the early morning sun. I'm suddenly nervous, my throat dry. I study myself in the rearview mirror, just a collection of lines around my mouth and dark circles beneath my eyes. I look like I slept in the backseat of a Toyota.

In a dreamlike daze, I drift across the street, take up

position outside Her door. I don't want to buzz up to Her place, for reasons I probably don't want to admit to myself. Catching Her in the act and all of that. Delivery drivers unload boxes from their trucks, businessmen hustle to the El train. No one notices me. Her door swings open, but it's just another guy in a suit and power tie. He eyes me suspiciously as he goes on his way, arrogantly slinging a backpack over his single-breasted jacket. Prick. Nothing happens for a long while, and I shift my weight from one foot to the other, my hands jabbed deep in my pockets. What am I doing here? Maybe this is a terrible mistake. Maybe I am going crazy again. Another motion at the door, but it's just an old lady, stern and buttoned-up in her sadness. She looks like a principal or something.

An hour goes by, I think. People leave the building. None of them are Her. I stand there, sweating in my early morning mania. By now, everyone is awake at my parents' house. They know that I'm missing, have probably called my cell, have heard it ringing upstairs in the bedroom. They are probably worried about me. I am thinking that maybe I should find a pay phone, should let them know that I'm alive and only slightly insane. But then, the door of the building swings open, and I turn and she walks right into me. Textbooks fall to the street. In slow motion Her eyes look up, meet mine. Her face goes blank. The smile exploded across those wonderful lips. She buries Herself in my chest, wraps Her arms around my shoulders. She's shaking like a child, so small in my arms. It's everything I could've imagined it would be. Actually, that's a lie. It's even more.

"You came for me" is all she says. It's all she has to.

There are no apologies. No explanations. None are necessary, not now, probably not ever. The tears well up in Her big eyes. Somewhere deep inside me, something comes alive again. We go up to Her apartment, kissing on the stairwell. We go into Her bedroom. I go inside Her and stay there all day. The world spins along outside, the sun rises and sets, the streets go dark, the lights come on. The future is happening, but it can wait until tomorrow. Neither of us knows what will come next, or where we go from here, or even what anyone will say about us, but none of it matters. We've got each other right now.

Later that night, as she's taking a shower, I call my parents from Her phone. It was largely anticlimactic. They weren't even mad that I took my brother's car. Turns out John Miller had told them where I was going that morning, over breakfast and coffee in the kitchen. I never told him my plans, but he probably knew them even before I did.

17

O happy, blustery Chicago days, the sky getting heavier, the leaves changing colors. O endless fall nights, the wind getting colder, the stars brighter. Everything is beautiful when you are mindlessly in love, when you ignore your fears and doubts and focus hard on the here and now. We are inseparable again, she and I, making the scene at the bars, walking the campus of Columbia arm in arm. There are doubters, those who shoot us disapproving glances from across tabletops and crowded rooms, but they all seem insignificant and far away. Her friends aren't talking to Her anymore. The guys in the band just sort of nod in that knowing, weary way. None of them matter to us. I haven't had a rational thought for weeks now, haven't felt the need to worry. She does something to me, something no one else on the planet can do. She makes me normal, she makes me free.

We never even forgave one another for the past. It didn't seem important. We just picked up right where we left off, before it all went bad and I lost my mind. I haven't thought about the band in a long time, haven't felt the promise of the open road course through my veins. Everything goes into Her. We talk about getting married, we think up names for our children (I want to call my son Martin, she prefers Oliver). We are perfect and in love and we are making everyone around us sick. At night, when I lie next to Her in bed, sometimes I worry that I am delusional, that perhaps I am rushing things. My heart may be in the driver's seat at the moment, but my brain is still shouting directions from the back. Why? How? Really? But then she'll stir, will turn into me to protect Her from whatever bad dream she's having, and the doubting stops. I am a believer. I want to believe.

John Miller and I find an apartment in Bucktown, a slightly dingy place above a bar on Wabansia. When we had originally cooked up the idea of moving in together, we had envisioned our place as a sort of clubhouse/rendezvous point, a launching pad for our great adventures; we had plans for wild nights spent carousing and conquering, for weekday mornings spent sprawled out on the couch, for gluttony and sloth and adultery and all sorts of lesser, decidedly venial sins. Instead, she is basically over every single night, cooking us dinners, watching movies, playing three-person power hours. John Miller doesn't mind. He loves anyone who will make him a hot meal, and he especially loves someone who can handle their liquor. She can do both. They develop a rather amazing bond, like an overprotective brother and his kid sister, or one of those YouTube clips where a bear raises a kitten or something. One night, when we are all good and drunk, when nothing seems impossible and everything is unspeakably *right,* she is dancing in the middle of the living room to some old record, and he leans over and tells me, "I kin see why you love Her." He is my best friend. She is my girl. Our lives are simple and insular and beautiful. I don't even worry about how John Miller is going to pay his share of the rent. It doesn't seem all that important right now.

Of course, it can't last forever. Our manager is leaving me messages on my phone, "checking in" on me, ending each one with the promise (threat?) of "Talk to you soon." I never return his calls, hoping he'll just give up and go away. Instead, he starts calling more frequently, his voice getting increasingly nervous with each message he leaves. When we do finally speak, the conversation starts with broad, friendly generalities—*How are you?* and *What have you been up to?*—as if we're just beginning a fight and he's feeling me out. It switches gears when he asks how the other guys are ("I don't know," I tell him) or if I've been working on any new songs ("Not really," I sigh). He's getting frustrated now, telling me "the people at the label" are wondering if we're thinking of getting back into the studio anytime soon. His voice now has a corporate passive-aggressiveness. When I tell him no, he's silent.

After a few seconds he says, "Listen, I'm not going to try and force you guys to do something you don't want to do. But I want you to be aware of—to be cognizant of—the, uh, the—I don't want to say *pressure*—but the, uh, *suggestions* I'm getting from the label now. They want another record. They, uh, well, they believe the time is right, want to, uh, 'strike while the iron is hot' is what they're saying, and, uh . . ."

I stop listening. I already know how this conversation is going to end. I can try to fight it, but there's no point. They have the leverage, they have our signatures. My happiness is not in the best interest of their stockholders. We are commodities now, we are the down payment on some CEO's waterfront property. We are making another album.

Against my objections, it is decided. Even though I don't have a single thing written, we leave for LA in a week. We'll just write the songs out there, the label seems to think (and our manager insists). What could possibly go wrong? I haven't even thought about Ativan in a long time, but now, images of those little pills dance through my head. My brain will always get the best of my heart. Life sees to it.

The next week is morose. The skies over Chicago open up, as if someone up there is crying nickel-size tears. It rains for four days straight, and eventually even the sewers get sick of it, because they start spitting the water back out. Those who are more carefree have taken to the flooded streets and formed an armada. Her and I just stay in bed. There's no point to doing much of anything. The city is permanently cast in a suspicious green light that's not quite haunted, but definitely considering it.

The day of my departure draws closer, and now she and I are in my bedroom at the apartment, filling my suitcase with clothes for my journey to the West. I never even got the chance to unpack my stuff from when I moved out of my parents' house, so I just move clothes from one container to another. Life is just a series of containers, and ultimately, you end up in one. I am tossing old socks and T-shirts into the case, and she is removing them, folding them into neat little packages, putting them back in the case in perfect stacks. I stop for a second and watch Her work, and it makes me smile. She is just like my mother, I think to myself.

I don't want any of this to end; I don't want to leave Her again because I am afraid of what will happen when I do. We are eternally being pulled apart. Eventually, it becomes impossible to put things back together again. We have to trust and believe in one another, have to have faith. But she promises me that she is okay with my going to Los Angeles, understands that this is just part of life. She swears she's not worried about us. She is being brave. She has Her brave face on now—chin jutted out, lips pursed, eyes serious—as she's folding my underwear. She notices me watching Her and smiles.

"What are you looking at?" she asks.

What *am* I looking at? My future wife? The mother of my children? The person I was put on this earth to find? Yes. But saying any of that seems silly when she's folding my underwear.

"Nothing, just watching you," I say, then, after a long pause, add, "Sometimes I wish I could be invisible so I could watch you do stuff like this all day long. Observing you in your natural habitat, like on a nature show."

"You're going to need a longer lens, then." She laughs. She is being brave again.

"Hey . . . you know I don't want to do this, right? You know I don't want to leave you, and I wish you could come out there with me—"

"I'll fly out." Her eyes are looking down at a shirt she is folding. "I'll be out as soon as finals are over. Only a couple of weeks."

"I know, but . . . I don't want to be apart from you. And I know it isn't fair. So I want to promise you something. I promise that this is it for me. After we make this record, I'm done. And I'm not just saying that for you, it's for *me* too. I love you and I want to be with you forever, and I don't want anything to get in the way. So this is the last time I'll leave you. Do you understand?"

"Of course I do. But don't go making promises like that. I don't want you to," she says, trailing off slightly. "This is a chance for you, for the band, to fulfill your dreams. To go to LA and make a record in a big studio, to have someone else pay for it. This is what you've been working for. And I don't want you to give it up because I know someday you'll regret it. So don't make any promises."

"You know I'd give it up for you. You know I would. In a second."

"I know."

In that instant, the room feels massive, like we're standing on opposite sides of a canyon, and suddenly I can feel the anxiety creeping up my legs, wrapping its tentacles around my bones. But then she walks across the void, Her little feet tiptoeing around the boxes, Her hips sashaying side to side, a sly smile on Her face. She pulls me toward her, tells me, "You're sweet, you know that?" I crack a smile. Life will not tear us apart this time. Our hearts will see to it. We make love on the bed, with an audience of cardboard boxes watching intently. It is kind of sexy.

18

We're inmates at the Oakwood apartment complex, which our label rep lovingly refers to as "the Cokewoods." The sign on the gate is emblazoned with the three most gorgeous words, FULL RESORT AMENITIES, written in a looping, regal script. But that makes the place sound much nicer than it is. Oakwood is where movie studios and record labels house "talent" whenever they're in Los Angeles working on a project. I believe the correct term for the place is "temporary furnished and serviced apartments," or at least it says so in the brochure. But basically, it's where child almost-stars and has-beens-in-the-making do tons of cocaine (hence the nickname) and then fuck each other in the hot tubs. It's a twenty-four-hour nightmare, fueled by those little white lines, full of silicone-injected blondes and men with bizarrely white teeth. And kids, C-list actors from Disney shows, most not a day over fifteen, wandering around with sadness in their eyes and white powder around their nostrils. Terrible house music is always playing by the pool. It's brutal.

We spend every minute indoors, hiding from the zombies that prowl the place, and though we should probably be working on songs, we basically amuse ourselves by calling our rep—a nice girl named Jen-with-Two-*N*'s (that's how she introduced herself when she picked us up at LAX, so we refer to her only as such)—and begging her to come and save us. She picks us up in an SUV, and we drive around Los Angeles, up to the top of Mulholland Drive, which probably looks a lot like the movie I never saw. The garages here are twice the size of most people's houses. We get out of the car and marvel at the view, but Jen-with-Two-*N*'s says we can't stay up here for long because homeless people hide in the bushes and wait for you. Imagine it: the richest homeless people in the world.

Up there at the top, you can see the smog hovering above the valley, as if it's trapped in there and can't get out. In the distance, the skyscrapers of downtown Los Angeles are barely visible through the yellowish haze. The suburban sprawl fans out in all directions, split-level houses clinging to the cliffs, block after block of apartment buildings, huddled together for safety. When I think about the California suburbs, it brings to mind the Mansons, not the Cleavers. Los Angeles is like hell only with more pretty people. You would think all the plastic would melt out here in the desert heat.

We tell Jen-with-Two-*N*'s that we want to see the water, so she begrudgingly takes us down to Santa Monica (a trip that, thanks to the traffic, takes roughly twenty-two hours), where we walk out to the end of the pier and watch the old men cast their reels into the Pacific.

They stand there in silence, listening to ball games on the radio, buckets full of minnows between their feet, until one of them gets a tug on his rod, then in a sudden burst of excitement, in a whirlwind of yanking and frantic reeling and cursing in Spanish, the rod bending and threatening to break in two, the old men shout instructions, and everyone holds his breath until eventually the old man is victorious, and he pulls a huge fish out of the ocean, shiny and electric and wriggling, and a great cheer goes up along the pier, and the old man accepts congratulations from his fellow fishermen, and maybe takes a drink or two, and tourists snap photos of the wide-eyed, silvery fish while the pelicans watch with hungry eyes. Everyone wants a piece of the action.

We roll up our jeans and walk on the beach, while women in Lycra sports bras jog by, pushing their babies in three-wheeled sports strollers. Men do yoga in the sand. We look ridiculously out of place, with our pegged jeans and pale skin in the early evening sun, but nobody even looks in our direction. Everyone is lost in their own little world, which is kind of the way things are out here. Los Angeles is a great place to disappear because people don't notice anyone but themselves. Jen-with-Two-N's is standing up on the boardwalk, furiously typing away on her BlackBerry. You can tell she's getting a little annoyed with us, probably because she has to go back to her boss with daily status updates, has to say stuff like "Today they all went to Santa Monica and watched old men fish." Ledgers are shifted, and the stockholders are getting restless. I expect a phone call from our manager any day now.

The songs are coming along, albeit slowly. Martin and I are sharing a "temporary furnished apartment" at Oakwood, and we stay up late writing lyrics and melodies, while Sodom and Gomorrah rage on outside our windows. He and I have got close again since we've been here, mostly because we're the two sorest thumbs of the lot. Neither of us wants to be here, trapped inside our earnestly appointed little cell, and both of us are missing someone back home in Chicago, so we're penning joyous little numbers about that. He has always been a sweet, good-natured guy, with kind eyes and an infectious smile. He is bringing out the best in me, which is why I don't mind writing with him. But there is also a more selfish reason: I see in him a way out because I believe he could carry this band forward when I leave. And I'm most definitely leaving, as soon as this record is done. He doesn't know that yet—none of the guys do—but I figure now is probably not the best time to tell him.

When I'm not writing, I'm talking to Her. So far everything is okay, our lives remaining in sync despite the distance between us. John Miller helps out, as he's sort of become Her unofficial guardian in my absence. He is a constant in both of our lives these days. It also helps that Her and I have developed a routine, one born out of my insomnia. I am always awake at 5:00 a.m., which is 7:00 a.m. back home in Chicago, so we do a video chat, me wide-eyed and sleep-deprived, spouting all kinds of nonsense, Her laughing tiredly and getting ready for school. Eventually, I fall asleep (usually around 6:00 a.m.), when she is in class. By the time I'm awake again, she's back home, and we spend the next few hours sending texts to one another. Then, at around 11:00 p.m., she gets ready for bed, and we do another video chat. She brings the computer to bed with Her, and I talk to Her until she falls asleep. Some nights, she forgets to sign off, so I sit in Los Angeles and watch Her sleep in Chicago, grainy and barely visible in the dark, Her breathing mixing with the sounds of the city, in that bedroom I know so well. Eventually, our connection times out and she freezes on my computer screen, no more breathing or movement, so I swallow a few Ativans and go back to doing whatever distracts me from my loneliness . . . usually this means staring out the window at the action in the hot tubs, or maybe walking down to the vending machines for no particular reason, except that my brain is sort of humming and fuzzy and warm and it's telling me I need to get some of that California air, to breathe it in and let it cool my system. So I stand outside in my hoodie, drinking a can of soda, my eyes swooshing around in a haze, over to the glimmering taillights on the Hollywood Freeway, across the night to the fences of Universal City, or down to the pitiful Los Angeles River. Behind me are the Hollywood Hills, all pocked and mysterious in the moonlight, and beyond that, the Forest Lawn cemetery, the final resting place of silver-screen stars. Famous ghosts in there. One night I got all freaked out because I thought I heard a coyote over in the bushes, and Jen-with-Two-N's had told me that tons of them were up here, and that they kill people's pets at night. I'm thinking of switching meds, for the record. Ativan isn't doing it for me anymore. Or it's doing it too well. I'm not sure. Anyway, eventually 5:00 a.m. rolls around again and we do another video chat, I watch Her leave for school, and the process starts all over again. I'd say we spend roughly half the day talking to each other, yet we say absolutely nothing of substance. I am strangely okay with this. We are both nervous. We both see the writing on the wall. We are both choosing to ignore it.

She never flies out to see me because Her mother conveniently gets sick just as finals are over. Her mother looks like a skeleton. She is always sighing and moaning about something, always struggling against someone. She is always the victim. She and I don't like each other that much. When she goes back into the hospital, that means no visit to Los Angeles, which only further puts a strain on things. Now whenever we talk, she's usually standing in the hallway of some Chicago hospital and I'm peering out my window at the suntanned silicone of LA. She is reading me pamphlets about Copaxone and Avonex, I am listening with an Ativan on my lips. There are long periods of silence. We are living in alternate universes. I suspect Her mother did this on purpose. She always hated me.

So, with nothing to do and no one to look after, John Miller decides to head West. I have the record label pay for his flight. First class. Fuck them. He lands at LAX and steps out into the smog and sunshine and feels a shudder run up his knotty Southern spine. His quest for adventure has taken him to the end of the continent, to the end of the world. He has reached his spiritual home, his Mecca. Here he will officially become the Disaster. He shows up at Oakwood with a canvas pack slung over his shoulder (a definite improvement over a Hefty bag), tells me he's arranged to have "the gays from downstairs" watch the apartment while he's gone. His return flight is booked for two weeks from now, but he'll change that. His eyes are manic, filled with fire and heritage and a million bad intentions.

"Now," he drawls, "why don't you show me whut this town is all about?"

We spend the next week haunting the hipster bars in Silver Lake, the velvet-rope Hollywood spots with one-word names, the terrible Red Bull–and-vodka joints on Sunset. We pass out in the achingly minimal lobbies of hotels, DJs playing down-tempo-chill-out bullshit behind black-lacquered booths. We waste away poolside at the Roosevelt, we get invited to a bungalow party at the Chateau Marmont, where we watch the cast of some primetime make bad decisions. The Disaster swears some sitcom actress made a pass at him, but I didn't see it. There are pills and powders and pot so strong it makes your head ring, black eyeliner and smeared lipstick. Half-smoked cigarettes slowly expiring in ashtrays. Blurry photographs of kissy-faced model/actresses. Bottles and black light. Endless nights and afterthought days. We have kidnapped Jen-with-Two-*N*'s, mostly because we need a designated driver, and she is eternally hammering away on her BlackBerry, though after a few days, her hope of rescue begins to diminish, and one night she gets so drunk I have to drive back to the Oakwoods. She and the Disaster made out in the hot tub while the living dead cheered them on. Everything is falling apart.

I still don't belong here—I'm an outsider, a periph-
eral character—but some nights I feel I can see my future
playing out in front of me, in the dark corners and the
bathroom stalls, the sparkling cleavage of sad starlets,
the orchids in the hotel lobbies that make everything
smell like a funeral parlor. I stand at the valet line in the
dusty, early morning light of Los Angeles, when Sunset
Boulevard is bathed in a somber, shimmering red, like a
well-trod trail of rubies leading to heaven, and I think
to myself that one night I'll follow that path off into the
ether. The Great Ghost of Death is everywhere out here,
in the Marilyn impersonators on the street corners, the
stoic murals of James Dean, the stars on the Hollywood
Walk of Fame. It reverberates off the hills, vibrates down
into the valley, colors the yellow air that we breathe. It's
why the young and famous party with reckless, feckless
abandon: they're either trying to forget about dying or
resigned that their death is inevitable. When I am drunk
and spun out on Ativans, I fear that I too am destined
to die in this town, out in these hills, with the ghosts of
singing cowboys and Marlboro men and about a million
rock-star corpses guiding me into the light, my body left
to the coroners and the coyotes. Everything is coming
undone.

I am thinking this as I sit in the bungalow at the Chateau, the party whirling around me, the Disaster crashing
over furniture, careening down the hallway, terrifying
everyone in his path. I am thinking about death—Belushi
overdosed in one of these bungalows, someone had
just told me—when she calls, and I answer with a roar

because I can barely hear myself over the din of Young Hollywood's demise.

Her voice is faint and distant on the other end because she's whispering in the hospital hallway. "Hi, hello? It's my mom, she—"

People are shouting, I can't make out a word she's saying. I tell Her to hold on as I climb over the arm of the sofa, snake my way down the hallway, force my way through a crowd of beautiful people at the door. I hear Her ask, "Where *are* you?" All I can say is "Hold on . . . sorry . . ." Finally I am outside by the pool, and I plug my ear with my finger and pour honey into the receiver, cooing, "Sorry, honey . . . sorry about that. How are you?"

I am beyond drunk. I do not realize how bad this could be.

"Where *are* you right now?" is all she says.

"Oh, I'm at a party . . . at the Chateau Marmont." I'm still trying to pull off the babe-in-the-woods routine. "The place where all the celebrities stay. John and I got invited to a party here, and it's—"

"You're at a party?" she shoots back, probably scaring some orderlies.

"Yeah . . . I . . . is that okay?" I tremble, the blood slowly draining from me. Assorted fabulous folk, previously lounging poolside, sunglasses on in the middle of the night, now turn their attention to me, the ratty outsider slowly drowning in the deep end. I hadn't noticed that I was still shouting. The gallery laughs condescendingly.

"What? I don't care. Listen. My mom . . . it's not

good." Her voice is flat like an out-of-tune piano, lifeless like a corpse on a slab. "The doctors say she hasn't been responding to the medicine . . . the new medicine, the Copaxone . . ."

Silence. I am missing my cues.

"The Cofazone?" I shout again, earning more stares from the people around the pool. I am out of my mind.

"No, COH-PA-ZONE. It's not working, and she's starting to shake more and more now. So they say that, maybe they've run out of options. They say there's not much else we can do now . . ."

Her voice cracks at the end of the sentence, trails off down the haunted hallway. I figure I am supposed to be compassionate now, even though I'm not certain it would be a bad thing if we *were* out of options, even though Her mother's been out of options at least five times in the past and has inexplicably survived, even though I am a terrible person. So I say I'm sorry because that's what people say in situations like this. I decide to whisper the words so maybe they'll carry a bit more meaning, but she says nothing back. Maybe whispering was a bad choice due to the shitty cell-phone service out here. I clear my throat and repeat the apology more audibly. She says she heard me and then asks if I could come back to Chicago for the weekend, because she needs me there, because she is confident Her mom is going to die any second now. I tell Her I'll see what I can do.

More silence. The heavy, awful kind. The worst kind.

"Okay. Well, I'm going to go back in with her," she says, completely deflated, betrayed by the man she loves when she needed him the most. "Call me in the morning, okay?"

"I will. I love you."

"I love you too."

Then she hangs up. Everything is broken now. Everything is falling into the Pacific Ocean. I stand by the side of the pool for a minute, thinking about the ghost of John Belushi. The empty lounge chairs. The candles flitting in the breeze, lilting back and forth on the breath of the Great Ghost. Everyone has gone back to ignoring me now, returning their attention to hastening their inevitable demise. I am nothing to them once again. I am a ghost. One more Ativan goes down my throat. I go back to the bungalow, back to the clamor and the clatter and the cocaine. Back to the business of death. Girls are locking hips and lips. Guys are shouting and snorting. That prime-time actress is balanced on the arm of an Eames chair. She looks like an angel.

19

I fly back to Chicago for a week. Have a minor panic attack on the ride to LAX. Take three Ativans to settle myself down. This is becoming a daily occurrence. When I land at O'Hare, no one is there to greet me. I take a cab to my apartment, realize I don't have my keys, make the driver take me to my parents' house. My mom asks me if everything is okay. I tell her I don't know and go to sleep in my old bed. I wake up a day later, my cell phone on the floor, the message light blinking violently. I go to Her apartment. Her bed isn't made. Nothing is sadder than an unmade bed. We go see Her mother in the hospital. We hug awkwardly, and I can feel her shoulders twitching as I hold her. Spend the next few days wandering the hallways, poking my head into mysterious, darkened rooms, eating french fries in the cafeteria. I smoke cigarettes with Her outside the emergency room. We don't talk about much. At night, I hold Her while she sleeps. We don't have sex. Her mother doesn't die. All in all, it was a bad trip.

As I am waiting for my return flight, I am suddenly and

inexplicably overcome with terror. I shouldn't be leaving. I should stay here where I am safe. The floor goes out from underneath me. My pupils become black holes. I am shaking and sweating, my stomach is tumbling. Tears are streaming down my face. I fumble for my phone, call Her to come save me. She tells me to calm down, that she will call me when she's done talking to the doctors. My flight will be gone by then, and so will I. She tells me to take my medication and says she has to go. Silence on the other end. I was calling for a little compassion. I got none. I am aware of the irony of the situation.

I swallow a handful of Ativans—who's counting anymore?—and crash out on the plane. I arrive back in Los Angeles, call the Disaster to see if anyone died while I was gone. He asks me if I'm all right. I tell him I don't know and hang up. I call Her to say I made it to LA. Voice mail. When I get back to the Oakwoods, I close my blinds and crawl into bed. I pull the sheets over my head and try to imagine what it would be like to be dead. The air-conditioning kicks on. Outside, silicone and meat are stewing in the hot tub. I fall asleep flat on my back, my arms at my side, like a cadaver. I wake up a day later, when Martin starts pounding on my door. He comes into my room and sits in the corner, asking me if I feel okay, if I need a doctor. He doesn't say it, but I can tell he's worried that I've gone off the deep end. I don't blame him. I'm worried too. I can't even begin to explain what's happening to me.

I am informed that some doctors in Los Angeles can get you anything you need, no questions asked. They will even come to your "temporary furnished and serviced

apartments" if necessary. They are quick with the diag-
nosis and even quicker with the prescription pad. I figure
now is as good a time as any for a consultation. The Disaster knows a guy who knows a guy, so I have him summon
a doctor to my bedroom. A slick-talking guy, with a wide
tie and a white smile. Tan. Pager on his belt. He looks like
he just stepped off the set of a soap opera. Maybe he did.
It doesn't matter all that much. He listens to me talk for
a while, then whips out the pad and gives me a script for
Zoloft. The little, blue miracle workers. He doesn't even
ask if I'm taking any other medications, probably because
he knows the answer already. Or he doesn't care. If only
Chicago had doctors like him. As he's leaving, he gives me
his pager number, tells me to call if I need anything. I am
now officially taking meds for anxiety and depression. I
am now officially under his care.

A week or so later—who's counting anymore?—I am
wandering the aisles of a bookstore in a haze, and during
a momentary break in the clouds, I find myself staring at
The Pill Book, "the illustrated guide to the most-prescribed
drugs in the United States," according to a blurb on the
cover. I have always liked illustrations, so I buy it. Thou-
sands of pills are listed inside, of every shape and size,
potency, ability. They have fantastically foreign-sounding
names, such as Abacavir and Norvasc and Zaroxolyn,
that clog the tongue and bunch the lips. Betatrex and
Cerebyx, Lorazepam and Mevacor, Questran and Ryna-
tan. My old friend Ativan. My new nemesis Copaxone.

Anoquan. Decadron. Guaifenex. Norethin. Roxicet. War-
farin. Names that recall distant galaxies hovering on the
rim of space. Placid resort towns in Arizona. Snow-dotted
villages in New England. Sterile stops on the sterling-
silver superhighway of tomorrow. Misty, quartz-powered
home worlds of superheroes. Letters seemingly chosen
at random to make words—new words, a new language,
a new world. Alphabet soup. Flurries. Each of them is a
unique, little snowflake. Each of them is beautiful.

I hide the book under my mattress, like it was an old
copy of *Playboy* and my parents were in the next room.
I lock the door to my bedroom and read it at night. My
pulse quickens with each page I turn. My eyeballs flutter
in the dim light of my Oakwoods apartment. I hope my
mom doesn't walk in on me. Snorted, swallowed, or shot
into my stomach, every pill represents a new opportunity,
a new neuron-frying, serotonin-searing adventure for me
to embark on. There are dosage guides and lists of possible side effects. Food interactions. Generic equivalents for
the penny-pinchers. Overdose warnings too, but I usually
ignore them. It's a step-by-step guide to self-medicating,
sort of like *The Anarchist Cookbook* for manic depressives.
I am no longer aware of how many different pills I am
taking, but I find myself paging the Soap Opera Doctor
at least once a day. He doesn't seem to mind. He's seen
hundreds of guys just like me, nobodies from the middle
of nowhere who show up in his town and promptly fall
apart. I'm just following the script, having my first melt-
down. Call me a cliché. I probably won't even notice. My
eyelids are always heavy. Things are easier this way. No

talking, no feeling, no pain. Just a handful of prescriptions and the occasional suspicious look from the pharmacist. Days blur into nights. Dull, warm sunsets become hazy, fuzzy sunrises. Los Angeles begins to disappear into a pharmaceutical haze. And I go with it. Sometimes, I even admit that I'm sort of *enjoying* all this. This is what I am supposed to be doing, after all.

I haven't slept in a while now. My sentences are running like they just want to get away from whatever's behind them. I've been writing Her e-mails with no beginning or ending, just middles, deep blue oceans of letters and words with no feeling or meaning. They don't make any sense at all. I start calling my mom's work voice mail at two or three in the morning, leaving fifteen-minute-long messages about how I'm doing okay. I think I am making breakthroughs and announce my brilliant theories. I try to bring her to her knees. I try to say something that will eclipse all the love she has ever given me; something so big that it will open up a new perspective for her and set her free. That's the least that I owe her. Most of the time, I delete the messages after I listen to them once or twice. Maybe one of these times, I will leave one for real.

I lie in bed and look through the personals in *LA Weekly* to see if anyone is lonelier than me. I like the ones in the *Weekly* because they're the craziest and most desperate, and in Los Angeles, that's saying something. There is an art to decoding them—it's all semantics and verbiage— though it helps if you're screwed up and on the brink of collapse as I am: "Still Searching" means "Confused and

Lost." "Free-Spirited" means "Crazy, or Even Possibly Psychotic." "Thrill Seeker" means "I Like to Get High." And "Adventuresome" means "Nymphomaniac." The personal ads in Los Angeles are the saddest in the world. At least in cities like New York or Chicago there is hope, born primarily out of crowding—after all, you could be standing next to your soul mate on the train *right now,* or folding your unmentionables next to him or her at the Laundromat downstairs *next weekend*—but LA has nothing but great, impersonal distance, millions of lives spread across valleys and vistas, snarling lanes of traffic, sprawling, stuccoed apartment buildings. You could go an entire day without speaking to another living soul. People in LA are decaying and dying, breaking apart at the seams, scattered and hidden from view. All they're looking for is someone to be miserable with. Odds are, they will never find that person. Geography and traffic patterns will see to it. I laugh about this every time. To myself.

Everyone around me is worried, everyone is looking at me with watery eyes and a concerned face. Speaking to me in sentences that trail off into silences. But the thing is, this all seems to be *working*. My brain has always been my enemy, and I've spent much of the past decade warring against it, with therapy and razor blades and bad behavior, with precision-guided prescriptions that targeted specific regions. Serotonin smart bombs and the like. I was prepared to fight this war forever, even if deep inside I knew I could never win it. There were civilian casualties (she was certainly one, many times over). Unexploded ordnances. Violations of the Geneva Convention. It was bad. Now—thanks to my new regimen of meds—my brain and I have entered into a new era of diplomacy. There are no bullets or bombs, no carnage, just man-made medicine, warm clouds of inhibitors and blockers that act as demilitarized zones. We are at armistice. We have secured peace in our time. Now every day is warm and soft, every minute feels like the time on an airplane just before takeoff, when the cabin becomes pressurized and your body is slowly being rocked back and forth, when you are teetering on the verge of sleep, when the voices of your fellow passengers blur and become part of the background, muted, soft, and sad. You close your eyes and drift away, and when you awaken, you are someplace else entirely. A new city, a different time zone. This happens to me almost every day, though usually I find myself standing on the pier in Santa Monica, or strolling down the boardwalk in Venice. No recollection of how I got here. No worries. I don't even have to adjust my watch.

We begin working on the record. I am barely in the studio, preferring instead to spend my days either transporting around Los Angeles or buried beneath my bedsheets, shades drawn on my windows. I don't do anything halfway. On this particular morning, I am hiding from the sun, neither alive nor dead . . . a zombie in training, when my phone rings. It's Martin on the other end, asking if I feel like coming down to the studio today. I tell him maybe, and he says it's been nearly a week since I've done any work. This is news to me. I tell him I think he's mistaken, and he assures me he's not. I hang up, take another pill, and go back to staring at the ceiling. The sunlight makes a prism above my head. The shades are fluttering in the artificial air. We have been cleared for takeoff. Then the phone rings again, and I stare at the number. It's our manager. I have been expecting this call for a while now. Eventually, someone was bound to tell him about this. I sit up in bed and clear my throat, answer.

"What are you doing?" he asks, though it's clear from his tone that he's not interested in hearing the answer.

"Hey, hey, man," I mutter, my voice still buried beneath the covers. "I, uh . . ."

"What the fuck are you doing?"

"I'm just in, uh . . . I'm in bed. I don't know why."

"I know why you are. You do too," he says, losing a bit of steam now. "Look, I—I'm not going to tell you how I know about the pills. It's not important how I know, it's not important who told me . . ."

He doesn't have to tell me. I know Martin called him. Martin panics easily. He is a good friend.

". . . that's not the issue here. The issue is the pills. And, uh, and getting you some help. I'm not judging you, I'm not asking why you're taking so many, that's not the issue either. The issue is, uh . . ."

The issue doesn't matter. He is going to want me to see another shrink. Some industry vet, someone who's been through the wars, seen the best and brightest burn out and fade away. Someone with a dangly earring, I bet.

". . . the issue is the band. And what your little, uh, little episode is doing to it. And, of course, getting you healthy."

"Of course," I say, though I'm not sure why.

"So, I want you to go talk to someone. He's a good guy. He helps people like you get through, uh, through situations like this. He comes recommended, of course."

"Of course."

"So I've e-mailed him and he's going to be in touch. I want you to go see him." New York traffic rattles in the background. Our manager is talking to me on the street. "Look, the band is one thing, but, uh, it's not the only thing, you know? Like I said, I'm not judging you, but I am, uh, you know . . ."

I do know. I just want him to say it.

". . . I'm worried about you. I want you to be okay." He shifts tone to make it clear that he's wrapping up this call. "So . . . go see him. For me. Would you do that?"

I tell him I will. He hangs up feeling satisfied with himself, thinking he has swooped in and saved the day. I imagine him taking a confident swig from his coffee. He is a good friend. I have a lot of them, even if I don't realize it. Despite overwhelming desires to the contrary, I get out of bed, pull on a hoodie, and head down to the studio, for the first time in a week. I leave most of the pills under my pillow, though I'm not sure why I'm even hiding them anymore. A couple of girls in the Oakwood hot tub whisper as I pass. They probably assumed I had died up in my room. It is bright and sunny and eighty-five degrees, but I am freezing. My hands are sweaty, my face is ashen. I begin life as a functioning addict not because I want to, but because I have to. I owe it to the guys, to our manager, to Her. We've come too far—from the KoC halls in Arlington Heights to the end of the continental United States—to give up now. I'm not about to call it a revelation, but it's close. Most times, revelations come when you least expect them.

When I enter the studio—a big, plush place with platinum records lining the halls and cocaine buried in the fibers of the carpets—the receptionist doesn't recognize me, and I have to be buzzed in by an engineer. No one says a word to me, trying hard to maintain that well-crafted vibe of *professionalism,* but they clearly didn't expect to see me back here. This record is being made in *spite* of me.

My hands shake a bit when I pick up my guitar. It feels impossibly heavy around my neck, like a weight I can't bear to hold. After a few minutes, the heft goes away. My guitar feels like a weapon again. Suddenly the pills and the sorrow and the flight towers don't seem to matter all that much. I don't know why. Martin whispers that he's sorry. I tell him not to be. I play along to a track, fumbling the beat a few times before getting it right. Behind the glass, our producer looks at me with tender, worried eyes. I will not let him down. I will not let anyone in this room down. Not today, at least.

That night, with my pills staring at me from under my pillow, I write Her my first clearheaded e-mail in a long while. I apologize for making Her worry, I tell Her I'm feeling better, though I don't even try to explain why. I haven't quite figured it out myself. I include a passage extolling the virtues of love and sanity, compare Her to a lighthouse in a churning sea. My beacon. I am sure it will leave Her breathless. The next morning she replies with *You have a spot in my heart that could never be replaced*.

It makes me laugh just a little. It's funny the way people only say shit like that right before they replace you.

20

Big things are happening. We are finishing the record. We are mastering and mixing and multitracking, seated behind great boards, nodding our heads to the beat, using words such as *tone* and *pitch* and *low end* as if we were industry pros. The guys at the studio humor our requests. It's sort of funny.

We are due to leave Los Angeles in a few weeks, scheduled to fly to New York to play the record for the folks at the label, to have meetings and do press and assuage stockholders. A tour is being planned. It is all very professional. The idea of boarding an airplane and traveling across the United States terrifies me. All those mountains and lakes and cities, all those places in which to crash. I'm not sure where I picked up this fear of flying, but it's real and not going away. I'm not sure how I'll manage, but I'm trying to take things one day at a time. The shrink told me that. I'm meeting with him regularly now, and while I won't bore you with the details, he seems like a genuinely good guy. He tells me amazing stories about the guys in

Mötley Crüe going on drug binges and buying automatic weapons and barricading themselves in hotel rooms. He has seen it all. He is trying to get me to meditate with him, and we take drives down to secluded beaches, sit on mats, and watch the pelicans swoop up and down the coastline. And, yes, he does, in fact, have a dangly earring.

I haven't paged the Soap Opera Doctor in a few weeks. That doesn't necessarily mean that I'm cutting out all the pills, but, rather, that I'm refusing to refill my prescriptions. I say good-bye to the tandospirones that you can only get in China, and the buspirones and the eptapirones that made my head whirl. I watch as the Zolofts and Ativans and Klonopins slowly dwindle away, and when they finally disappear, all I'm left with is some Tylenol PMs. Enough of them will do in a pinch. Everyone is a little less worried about me. The Death Watch is officially over. No one is afraid to wake me up in the mornings anymore.

This is all happening when she decides to leave me. We had a fight after I told Her that things were going well with the band, that I was excited again and that I hadn't thought about quitting in a few weeks. I told Her that I was considering staying in Los Angeles and thought she should move out here to be with me. After all, I joked, it's closer to Berkeley than the North Side of Chicago. She didn't laugh. This was apparently the final straw. The next day, she is on the phone to me, saying she knew this day was coming, and that she couldn't sit by and watch me kill myself. She said we had been stuck in place and she owed it to Herself to move on. I didn't necessarily disagree with

Her. I can tell she has found someone else, probably some boring dude in one of Her study groups or something. Someone who wants to wear sweaters and drink expensive coffee and live around the corner from the food co-op. Someone who is into Freud and the unconscious self. Someone who is not me.

She only cries a little bit as she's telling me this, and only retches once, the phone clinking against Her teeth, Her tears echoing off the bathroom tile. It is a fairly low-key affair. She doesn't even wait for me to object, probably because she knows I won't. We are both too tired for grand gestures, both too weary to go on fighting. A year ago, I would've hopped on a plane and showed up at Her place with dynamite strapped to my chest and a list of demands in my hand. I would've begged for us to go back to the way we were—*or else*. Fuck hostage negotiating; I would've been romance's last terrorist. Love's last chance. Now, I can't even be bothered to whip up some fake tears. No one needs to die for this. We've grown up and grown apart. We haven't slept in the same bed in months now, not since I went back to Chicago, and she hasn't made any attempts to come out to LA, even now that Her mother is stable again (as I knew she would be). Love has long since left the building. It's not coming back. As we're saying good-bye, I wish Her good luck with the new guy, and just as she asks, "What does that mean?"—I hang up on Her. She doesn't call back. I don't blame Her.

That night, I don't stay up waiting for the phone to vibrate, as I've done after every single fight we've ever had. I don't call any of my friends in Chicago and tell them to keep an eye on Her, just in case she does anything stupid. I don't stare at myself in the mirror and think about cutting my wrists, about expressing my love for Her with some childish final act. I just accept what has happened as part of life; an inevitable step on the path to wherever; "rungs on a ladder," as my dad always said. She's gone. Good-bye. And all of that would be great if any of it were true. What I *actually* do is sit on the edge of my bed and stare at my alarm clock and realize that this is never going to work out, that she will never be with me as long as I am with the band, and that I can never have everything because life is unfair and God has it in for me. I will always be alone and unloved, no matter how many kids buy our albums or shout my name. I start to feel like I'm going to vomit, but I stop myself because it would've got all over the carpet and we probably wouldn't get our deposit back. I pull my knees to my chin, rock back and forth in an attempt to settle my stomach, and as I'm curled up, I realize that I'm nothing more than a frightened child, a scared little boy with tough-guy tattoos and a hollow snarl, and that no matter how much I like to think of myself as a die-hard romantic, I'd never have the guts to actually *die* for love. Sure, I'd flirted with the notion, had got some illicit thrills out of the Soap Opera Doc and his prescription pad, but I'd never dreamed of going all the way. And that made me a phony, a liar. A coward. So right then and there, I decide to make a life change: I am going to die. I am practical about it. My shrink would be proud. I gather up every last pill in my possession—a fistful of blues and oranges and pale yellows—and swallow them all, lock myself in the bathroom, and break the mirror with my fist. I cut my knuckles up pretty good and blood trickles down my arm in bright red ribbons. It's full of oxygen and oozing and steaming hot. I begin to worry that all the pills I've been taking aren't letting the blood clot, so I freak out even more. My head is churning and there's a whole lot of blood now, so I crawl into the shower and start crying. White flashbulbs are going off in my eyes, and when I rub them, I get blood on my face. I turn on the water and sit there, getting soaked, watching the blood wash away from my knuckles, staining my clothes. Martin knocks on the door, asking me what's wrong. When I don't answer him, his voice gets louder, and he says my name, telling me to let him in, but I just put my head in my hands and feel the water run down the back of my shirt. I don't know how much time goes by—five minutes? An hour?—but then security comes and takes the door off its hinges, and a big, burly guy in a blue suit turns off the water and puts a towel around me while Martin and the rest of the guys stand in the living room. I sit on the corner of my bed, watching water pool around my sneakers while an EMT wraps my hand in gauze and shines one of those pocket flashlights in my eyes. He asks me what I've taken and I tell him I don't know, and his partner knocks around the pill bottles by my computer. I laugh because while my body is shivering, my head is so, *so* hot, and I ask the EMT if steam is coming out of my ears. He doesn't laugh and just goes "Uh-huhhhh" and calls me "sir" and asks me again what I've taken. The other guy is in the background holding up empty orange bottles, asking me if I took *all* of these, sir, did I take *all* of these, and I smile and lie and say, "Noooo." Both EMTs go back out into the hallway and talk to the guys, then come back into my bedroom and tell me I'm borderline and they think I should go down to the ER and have my stomach pumped, but since I'm borderline, they're leaving the decision up to me, and I tell them I'm fine and they respectfully disagree, tell me I should go with them, but I refuse again. They tell me that whatever I do, don't fall asleep, and as they're packing up their stuff, they tell the guys the same thing—whatever you do, don't let him fall asleep. They leave and the guys take turns watching me sit in a chair. Occasionally I go into the bathroom and throw up, and pink puddles are on the floor, my blood mixed in with the water, and one of the guys stands in the doorway and watches as I stick my head in the toilet. By noon, I feel better, and everyone decides it's probably okay for me to go to sleep, so I crawl into bed and sleep with my right arm elevated, since I'm still worried about the blood not clotting. When I wake up, I look at my damp clothes balled up in the corner and decide that I had probably overreacted. It was nice of the EMTs to come out though.

The Oakwood management, apparently concerned over the previous night's events, have called the record label and demanded I move out. They also put an official-looking letter on my front door—typed and on letterhead and everything—that mentions such stuff like property damage and "inherited risk." I think they're overreacting, and I go tell the property manager that if he really wants to clean up this place, he should start with the hot tubs, but he won't be swayed and I am shipped off to a hotel. The guys help me move, and our manager flies out to room with me. I can tell they are all annoyed with me, but they're masking it with serious talk and "general concern." Apparently, my little incident has morphed into "a cry for help," so now there's talk of my taking a little break from everything, since I'm clearly cracking up. I tell our manager that I'm fine, and I was just trying to get the blood off my hands, but he doesn't say anything, just nods. I am suddenly seeing the shrink with the dangly earring daily. He's gone serious on me now too. No more stories about Mötley Crüe and their AK-47s. He says I could've died from all the pills I took and that he can't believe the EMTs didn't take me to the psych ward for a seventy-two-hour hold. He tells me this is "very real" and that everyone just wants me to "get healthy." I shoot back that if people are really worried about my health, they should get me a gym membership. He actually laughs a little bit when I say it. He's okay in my book. People watch my every move, ask me how I'm feeling. I am under twenty-four-hour supervision. Jen-with-Two-N's is hugging me every time she sees me. Things are getting ridiculous.

All of this happens just before we are to leave for New York. Timing has never been my strong suit. We have a meeting to determine whether I'm okay to fly, and I lie on the couch and tell the guys I'm ready to go. They say I don't have to, that they can handle it, and that I should stay here and relax, but I won't listen. My hand is healing—the cuts are just tiny pink crosses on my knuckles now—and my head is actually feeling pretty clear, and I figure it's time to meet the shareholders. They're the ones who paid for this ridiculous trip, after all. I probably owe them an apology.

I believe I am fine until the night before we leave, when I find myself staring at my bags and googling stuff like *world's safest airlines*. We are not flying on any of them. I can feel panic starting to creep in, like ice water in my toes, so I take a couple of Tylenol PMs (the shrink said they were okay) and try to sleep. All night my bags sit by the door in an ominous black heap. At one point I swear I saw them move. Then it's morning and we're loaded into an SUV and sent on our way, and I pull my hood over my eyes and try to relax, try not to think about plummeting into the Rocky Mountains, but it's not working. I'm trying my best not to let the guys know, but I start shaking as we're going through security, and I can't take my boots off on my own. Martin helps, unknots my laces and places my boots on the conveyor belt. He tells me it's going to be all right. I don't understand why this is happening to me. I am embarrassed to be seen like this by my friends. I never wanted to be the anchor, I never wanted to pull us down. It seems that's all I'm doing these days.

As we sit on the runway, I can feel my pulse quickening. I'm having a hard time catching my breath, and tears are in my eyes. I wipe them away with my sleeve and try to focus hard on the in-flight magazine in my lap. I play with the tray table. I pray to God, even though I can't remember the last time He helped me out. I try to get my life in order, just in case this plane doesn't make it to New York. It's funny how fears hide inside other fears. The fear of airplanes hiding inside the fear of heights hiding inside the fear of highways hiding inside the fear of cars hiding inside the fear of elevators hiding inside the fear of leaving my room hiding inside the fear of living. Fear tries to own me. In the past, I had paid it rent by downing twenty milligrams of Valium and a Xanax and sleeping through flights, but now all I've got on me are some of the PMs, and they're not going to do the trick. A tranquilizer couldn't slow my heart right now.

I try to calm myself by thinking logically. I have read about calculated fears and irrational fears. The fear of flying is irrational. The odds of a fatal plane crash are something like nine in twenty-one million. It's like gambling, only you want the house to keep winning. Only nine in twenty-one million flights crash, but every single person who got on any one of those nine planes was thinking about a statistic just like that. Somewhere out there, someone pulls the lever on a slot machine and wins $30,000 on the first try. Somewhere out there, someone gets on a plane for the first time in his or her life and it crashes into the Atlantic Ocean.

Fear owns me because I let it. Because I obsess over it, name it, raise it, and nurture it to become perfect. It is one of the few things in my life that I can control. "It's just on this side of crazy," they say, but I'm not sure what side they're yelling that from. "You're losing it," they say, but I know I am, so technically speaking, I'm pretty sure I'm "giving it away," not "losing it." I decide before we take off that I need to hear Her voice, not because I miss Her but because I feel the need to get my life in order just in case the plane goes down. I call Her up and the phone just rings and rings, so I hang up and call again. This time she answers, but she's not in the mood to nurture my fears, to massage my neurosis, or to agree that God won't let this plane go down because there are kids on it. I don't really blame Her.

"You're losing it," she sighs.

"Whose side are you on?" I whine.

"There aren't sides. This isn't high school."

"There is me, and then there's everyone else," I shout into the phone. "Now pick!"

Sometimes when I am leaving, arguing with someone takes the place of saying a formal good-bye. Everyone on the plane is staring at me now. Kids have turned all the way around in their seats to look at the crazy man screaming into his cell phone. Their parents grab them and spin them forward again, as if I might infect them or something. The flight attendants are giving me concerned glances. I don't let any of that stop me. My life has veered off course. Has crashed into the mountain. I have become one of those people you see on daytime TV, the ones who shout obscenities at their exes and throw chairs around the studio. The ones who have Maury Povich do paternity tests for them. I am at the bottom. But still, I can go lower. I call Her a bitch and tell Her she has ruined me. I don't mention my incident from the other night, or the EMTs, but she gets the drift. The silence on the other end of the phone tells me she is searching for something to say to me. Something punishing. Something unforgivable.

"I hope your plane crashes," she spits.

Somewhere deep down, so do I, but I'm not lucky enough to be struck by lightning or to win the lottery. I'm not nine-in-twenty-one-million lucky. I hang up on Her just as the flight attendant tells me to turn off my phone, and after a perfunctory safety demonstration (as if any of it is going to help), we are roaring down the runway, picking up speed, rattling and straining and leaving the earth behind us. I am suddenly not afraid of dying anymore. I think it'd be a relief. And besides, no one would miss me if I were gone. I've burned all the bridges, collapsed all the walls.

Every time the plane bumps, I think of Her.

21

It's later. New York City on a February morning, in a winter that just won't quit. A hotel near Times Square, a wind that tears through the city streets, a cold that grips you and won't let go. Businessmen in trench coats, collars turned up, hustling to work. Neon signs just waking up. Or just going to sleep. Steam billowing up from somewhere down below, rank and heavy, the way you see in old movies. Coffee from a cart, in a paper cup, sugar congealed on the bottom. Me in a dream, taking it all in, skin blue, smoke pouring from my lips, hands dug in my pockets. My coat is somewhere in Chicago. My apartment, long vacant, probably burned to the ground. My life just as empty, and quite possibly as charred, the smoldering remnants put out on the street. Alone. Low. Months since I've shared a bed with another warm body, since I've put my hand on soft skin. An ad on a bus for laundry detergent, a smiling woman in a white robe, an angel here to rescue me. She disappears around a corner in a cloud of exhaust. Typical.

• • •

The guys are meeting the shareholders without me. They are playing them the record they made in spite of me. It's probably better that way. I am barely in the equation; I am a remainder at best. Maybe a decimal point. I have nothing to do, no place to be, and I can't bear to sit in my hotel room any longer, so I'm just wandering around the city, up and down the streets, with no coat on. It's almost as if I were on vacation, except I don't want to be here. I walk down to the water, stare at the old aircraft carrier rusting by the pier. It's called *Intrepid*. It is a floating metaphor. They've turned it into a museum, and tourists stop and take pictures. You can buy souvenirs up on the flight deck. New Jersey squats in the background, tiny rows of condominiums crowding the shoreline. The smokestacks of a factory. The darkness on the edge of town. Somewhere out there, Bruce Springsteen is waking up and having breakfast with his wife. Thinking of the Boss in his bathrobe makes me sad. The wind whips off the water, so I turn and walk off in the direction of nothing in particular. Eat breakfast at a diner even though I'm not hungry. Take a cab ride up and down the avenues, even though I've got nowhere to go. The driver looks at me in the rearview with his wild African eyes. I tell him anywhere is fine, and he dumps me on some corner on Eleventh Avenue, down by the Lincoln Tunnel. The air is thick with the smell of gasoline and the sound of mufflers. Huge buses hiss and downshift, full of passengers escaping the island. I can see the rear of the *Intrepid* off in the distance . . . I drove around for twenty minutes and only traveled ten blocks.

It's only around 10:00 a.m.; the meeting probably hasn't yet begun. I picture the guys sitting in some expansive lobby, being asked if they would like anything to drink. The Animal will say yes, because he always says yes. Martin will say no because he is polite. I laugh to myself and dig my hands even deeper in my pockets, start to walk back across the city, through the dingy parts of Ninth Avenue, with its old butcher shops and even older Italian restaurants, smoke-filled bars already open for business, bums hunched over in doorways, like another world, another time. Past the Port Authority Terminal, dank and smelling of urine, terrified kids from Indiana clutching their suitcases and looking up, always up, at the towering skyscrapers, some guy in a leather jacket trying to steal one of their wallets, everyone smoking. Beneath the shadow of the New York Times Building, white and regal and ramping up toward heaven. Back through Times Square, the tourists now posing for pictures with cops on horseback, the Ferris wheel in the Toys "R" Us lit up and slowly turning, laden with children. I'm nearly hit by a cab as I'm crossing Broadway, the driver throwing his hands in the air, me pounding the hood with my palms for added effect. Down to Bryant Park, old black men playing chess even in the cold, the grass slightly frosted even as the sun begins to poke through the February sky. Around to the front of the New York Public Library, those famous steps dotted with people, those famous stone lions sentinel and stoic, proud and vigilant. Even the pigeons won't go near them. Then over to Grand Central Terminal, cavernous and bustling, people pulling suitcases in every direction, children crying, voices and heels echoing around the space, off the marble floor, up to the constellations on the ceiling. The four-sided clock in the center of the room. The massive display board above the ticket booths, listing destinations (Katonah, New Canaan, Mount Kisco). Train tracks at the end of mysterious, gilded corridors, a temple full of secret passageways, and I follow one of them down below, see the trains snort and kick and whinny on the tracks, yearning to break free and *go,* and for a minute I think of getting on one—any one, it doesn't matter which—and heading north, but instead I just watch them fill with businessmen and women and babies, then shudder and depart, reminding me that there are other places in this world I could be, other places that are not here.

I look down at my watch and realize I've only killed about ninety minutes, and that the meeting is probably still going on, and that I cannot think of anywhere else to go, or anything else to do, and it sounds stupid, but in that instant it becomes clear to me that I am not in control of my own life, that none of us are, that the very *notion* of control is ridiculous. A man in a suit boards a train bound for White Plains, makes sure he catches the 7:05 so he will be sufficiently early for his appointment, and as the train departs from Grand Central, he is sitting in his seat reading his newspaper, feeling self-assured and calm, and everything is fine until that train hits a snag on the tracks—a broken joint in the rails, a loose bolt, who knows?—and derails, and he is thrown from his seat and killed instantly, dies with the same, smug look on his face. It was beyond his control. Something like this happens every day. Every minute. A train crashes. An airplane plummets to earth. John Miller's baby son dies. A land mine, an earthquake, a calamity. Life is merely a numbers game, a series of odds, and eventually we all lose. To think otherwise is foolish. But if we didn't, why would anyone ever bother getting out of bed in the morning?

Yet, I have spent the first twenty-five years of my life believing the exact opposite . . . that I was in control of my destiny, that fate is a myth, that there is no great book in the sky with my expiration date already written in it. I have fought and gouged and grabbed for control, have pushed everyone and everything aside to possess it. When I thought I had it, I vowed to never let it go, gritted my teeth and held on tightly, snapped at anyone who came close. That's how I lost Her. How I became an afterthought. There is no such thing as control. It's a red herring, a MacGuffin. It keeps us going, gives us false hope. Life is cruel and unfair and nothing more than a series of cosmic coincidences. We are powerless to stop it.

Right then and there, on the dirty subterranean platform, as the 11:37 off-peak departs for New Haven, I lose my mind. The water main bursts behind my eyes, and hot, salty tears come pouring down my cheeks, some of them flowing into my mouth, others landing on the filthy platform with a loud *splat!* Tears like I've never cried before. My pulse is pounding in my ears, it's so loud that it drowns out everything else. My legs go out from underneath me, and I am suddenly aware that I am sitting on the concrete, my knees pulled tight to my chest. People are staring at me, a woman nearly trips over me, and then a police officer grabs my shoulder, shakes me, and asks if I'm all right. It sounds as if he were talking underwater. I nod and wipe the tears from my eyes, tell him that my girlfriend was on that train, that she left and is never coming back. I am probably shouting right now. The officer clearly can't be bothered to arrest me—probably doesn't want to do the paperwork or something—so he pulls me to my feet and tells me to go cry somewhere else. I wipe my nose on my bare arm, leaving a long, glistening trail of mucus on my tattoos.

Now I am sitting in the second-floor waiting room, which is also sort of a food court, not to mention a good place for homeless men to masturbate. My head is in my hands, my ears are ringing. I'm not crying anymore, but that's mostly because I'm utterly, completely *drained*. There's nothing left inside of me. I am so alone, and so scared—terrified, for the first time in my life—because I've glanced behind the curtain, I've seen that no one is at the wheel. Not God, not anybody. There is no one left to believe in, nowhere left to go. We are all adrift, we are all lost, with nothing to put us back on course . . . because there *is* no course, there is only emptiness and space, numbers and ratios. That is a terrible way to look at life, but maybe it's also the most *realistic*. The most scientific. Albert Einstein did not believe in God. Neither did Carl Sagan. But they believed in *numbers*. Numbers are all that matter. God probably does not exist, and if he does, he's nothing more than an angry, old white man who spends his days shooting dice with the archangels, rolling sevens and elevens and making airplanes fall out of the sky, taking babies up to heaven for no reason in particular. He would not be the beatific, cloud-inhabiting superbeing we learned about in CCD classes. You would not like God if you met him.

Then again, maybe I am wrong. Maybe God is not a superstition. So I sit there and pray for Him to reveal Himself . . . for Him to show me a sign that He is really up there, that all of this misery is worth it in the end. These are the moments when He is supposed to reveal Himself, after all, when His followers are at their lowest. I pray to Him, beg for an answer. I wish this were easier. I want God in the form of a teen magazine "Is He right for you?" test, where I can turn the magazine upside down and look at all the answers to get the outcome I want, so I can cheat my way to peace of mind. I want it glossy. I want it easy. I've always believed in God. I'm just not so sure He believes in me.

It's like when Her and I used to fight late at night and then for the next six hours I'd watch my cell phone and wait for Her to call. That's what my belief in God has always been like. It is the most desperate, obsessive relationship I've ever had in my life. I want to stalk Him, to sit out on the street in front of where He lives and just know that He exists. I have been more unfaithful in this relationship than I have been to any of my exes. And it hasn't paid off at all; or maybe it has because I'm not dead. Yet. I open my eyes and look around the waiting room, searching for a ray of light or a dove or something.

A woman is eating a chicken sandwich. A janitor is mopping the floor. A homeless man has his hand down the front of his pants. Then, to my left, there is a child . . . a cherub-faced boy, in overalls, blond hair hanging down over his forehead, his eyes bright blue. A holy infant, so tender and mild, like the ones we used to sing about in church. He is looking at me with curiosity. I stare back at him, not knowing what to do. It occurs to me that I am looking directly into the face of God. I am peering deep into His azure eyes. There is a splendid silence. I lift my hand to Him, as if He were a spring and I am a parched man who has crawled through the desert. I reach for Him, an oasis, an illusion, a glorious thing. Then He starts freaking the fuck out, bawling, and His mother puts down the chicken sandwich and grabs Him by the waist. She lifts His tiny face to hers and coos, "What's the matter? What's wrong?" She wipes the tears from His tiny face. He wasn't God. He was just a little kid. God doesn't exist.

I wait for them to leave the waiting room, then I wobble to my feet and do the same, head back up into the massive windows and marbled arches of the main terminal. The light is shining down in the most theological way, and I understand that, once upon a time, someone built this entire building as an edifice to God's glory. I wonder if he or she knew what I know. Probably not. If they did, you can bet they never would've stacked two marble blocks together. I walk out onto the street, take a cab back to my hotel, shaken and broken, yet, on some level, *alive,* or maybe reborn, eyes wide, confident in the knowledge that I will probably never have a more depressing day in my entire life. And if I do, well, then I hope God or whoever strikes me down. I hope the universe pulls my number. Either way, the result will be the same.

22

I think everyone should go crazy at least once in their life. I don't think you've truly lived until you've thought about killing yourself. It's oddly liberating. I've called Her and apologized for my actions. Told Her I had gone off the rails a bit, but now I'm doing fine. Really, truly fine. She told me it was okay, and that I can call Her anytime I need to talk. She talks about school and Her job. Her voice is warm and comforting, like a blanket or the gentle hiss of the radiator on a cold morning. She sounded just like my mom. I am making peace with my past. I am moving on. I don't give a fuck anymore.

The shareholders liked the album. They heard a potential first single. And a second one too. It's coming out in May, I think. We're back in Los Angeles now—at least some of us are, Martin went back to Chicago—putting the final touches on the thing, doing overdubs and the like. Glossing it up a bit. I flew back here with no problems, made it all the way across the Great Plains and the Rocky Mountains without a sliver of anxiety medication, without a single tear. That chapter of my life is over. I'm tired of being afraid, and of being in control. I am officially on autopilot. I am leaving it all up to someone else. I am unchained and ready to live again.

I call my landlord back in Chicago, tell him that I'm going to keep my place there, and I use some of the money from the record advance to pay my rent for the remainder of the year. He sounds surprised to hear my voice, says he's glad to hear from me. I haven't been back to the apartment in something like six months, and I may never go there again, but I like the idea of having a space in the city, a hermetically sealed chamber, untouched since I left it so long ago. Cardboard boxes are still in my bedroom. I will probably never unpack them. That's okay.

I find another place in LA, up in the canyon, an old house with massive windows and a weathered veranda that overlooks the city, and the Disaster moves in with me. We are all alone up there, free to do stupid things, so we smoke tons of pot and get lost in the foothills, dry-mouthed and wandering among the scrub and the sago palms, leaping from rock to rock in the arid heat. At night, we explore with flashlights, twist our ankles in unseen crags, chase off coyotes with shouts and yips. We are like feral children, wild and free, unkempt. Except with drugs. And the handgun that the Disaster bought and now keeps tucked into the top of his jeans. He only shoots bottles at the present, setting them up on boulders and blasting them into oblivion, the sound of the gun echoing around the great walls of rock. He says he's going to bag a coyote one of these days. One time a jogger yelled at us, but for the most part we are left to our own devices. It's not too long before we stop wearing shirts, and the California sun begins to bake our skins. Imagine, a suntan in the middle of March.

We do a run of shows that takes us from west to east, headlining stuff now with a crew and catering and the like. Our very own bus. It's good to see the kids' faces again. To hear their voices sing along, not just to the old stuff but the new songs too. Our band is better than it's ever been before, we are survivors, we have made it through the tunnel and emerged into the light. We are on the cover of a magazine. We shoot a music video, again with a crew and catering and the like. Folding chairs with our names printed on the backs. Friends are texting me from Chicago to tell me they heard our song on the radio. My dad's clients are asking him if I could sign something for their daughters, since they're big fans and all. It occurs to me for the first time that I may actually be famous. You can't tell these kinds of things when you live in Los Angeles because *everyone* is famous out here. But in the Midwest, the Iowas and Ohios of the world, I can no longer go to the grocery store without having kids follow me, call out my name. I am signing autographs in the cereal aisle while the store manager apologizes. If we are out at a restaurant, we are asked to take photos with the waiters, to pose with the bartenders. Kids sit at tables near us, faking that they're snapping pictures of their friends, but tilting their cameras *just* enough to catch us in the background. Our manager is saying we might have to hire security pretty soon. I just laugh.

But back in LA, I'm just another guy. I can eat my dinners in peace. Only, in the weeks before our album comes out, my face starts turning up at bus stops, in the window of Tower Records, on a billboard down on Sunset. Suddenly, I am not just another guy. I am invited to parties at clubs, then after-parties in penthouses. It's just as it was all those months ago, when the Disaster and I ran roughshod over the city, only now we are *supposed* to be here. We are invited guests. Well, actually, I am, but the Disaster goes everywhere with me. I am beginning to be able to get us into any event, no matter how long the line outside, no matter how stone-faced the doorman. I have become Mr. +1. You should see my name there on the list . . . right there, yeah. And here's my friend. He gets in too. Okay? Cool? Thanks, man.

Eventually, we don't even have to bother with the list. The doormen know me by first name. They know I come with company. They unlatch the velvet rope and let us inside without a moment's hesitation. I am putting twenties in their pockets. They nod and say stuff like "Good to see you again" or "Have fun tonight." We usually do. One night we are in a club—a minimal, throbbing place with pure white light emanating from the floor, sort of like the Korova Milk Bar only without naked women for tables—sitting in the back, when the Disaster starts elbowing me. He nods across the room, and I look in the general direction and lock eyes with the most beautiful girl in the entire world—only for a split second, of course, then I avert my stare to the floor. I glance back up again, and she is smiling at me.

"Lookit that, man," the Disaster whispers in my ear. "She's lovin' you."

It would appear she is. She motions for us to come over and join her table, and the Disaster and I get up and make our way across the dance floor, nodding our heads to the beat, praying not to trip or spill our drinks. Everything is happening in slow motion. She is smiling at me and biting the corner of her lip. One of her friends whispers something to her and she nods and laughs. She covers her mouth with her hand. My heart is racing, I am understandably nervous.

"Hi," she shouts over the music. "Have a seat."

Her circle of friends parts and I am suddenly sitting right next to her, my hands nearly in her lap. She leans in close to talk to me, and I can see down her dress a bit, down into the promised land. I can smell her perfume. You can tell it's expensive. She is poured into something backless or strapless; either way, it's missing essential parts. And when I say *poured,* I mean more like half a glass—but definitely of something strong. I introduce myself and the Disaster, who is across the table, in between two girls who on any other night, in any other city, would've been the center of attention. They are gorgeous, otherworldly. Long necks laced with diamonds. They are slightly annoyed by the Disaster's presence, sitting upright and rigid, their eyes forward. He looks as if his head were about to explode. He has made it to the top of the mountain.

"I know who you are," she shouts in my ear. "I've seen your picture."

This is a key moment in all young celebrities' lives, the instant when they stop wondering and just *know* that they are different from the rest; that the world will stop for them. She figured this out a long time ago. Her skin shines as if it had been buffed with diamonds. Chances are pretty good it actually was. She is not mortal. She is something greater. How do you make small talk with someone like her?

"So . . ." is about all I can muster. "Hi . . ."

There is a pregnant hush around the table, everyone is craning their necks to hear me speak. I clear my throat and don't know what to say next. The pressure is mounting, my palms are sweating. She has reduced me to a panting, stuttering teenager. I am drowning.

"Relax." She smiles and touches my arm. "Have a drink."

She knows exactly what she wants, and she doesn't have time for games. She has seen and heard it all before. She is not impressed by any of it. Yet, as the night goes on, she seems positively *fascinated* by me, laughing at the stupid jokes I eventually make, leaning into my shoulder. She's like a cat toying with a mouse, batting me around with her paws, savoring the moments before she sinks her teeth in. The drinks flow, the music blares, the people stare, and suddenly it's two in the morning and she is asking me what I'm doing now, and if I'd like to come back to her place. She asks this merely as a formality: she knows I'm coming back with her, that we all are, and that we will stay for exactly as long as she wants us to, do anything she asks of us, because she is who she is, and that's the way it is. We leave the club, and photographers outside take her picture. They shout her name and ask her questions, but she doesn't even acknowledge their presence. It is as if they don't even exist to her, and she would walk *through* them if she could. Her friends form a protective barrier around her, usher her to a waiting SUV. The Disaster and I go with them, eyes wide, dumbfounded. You can see us in the background of some of the pictures. We look ridiculous.

She climbs into the passenger seat of the SUV—the photographers bringing their cameras low just in case she's not wearing underwear—and we pile in the back. Her friend is driving, driving right through the throngs of photographers, honking her horn almost as an afterthought. They pound on the windshield and snap away; the light from their cameras is blinding. Now I understand why celebrities are always wearing sunglasses. From the front seat, she is laughing, and she turns back and smiles at me.

"Sometimes they'll stick their feet under the tires on purpose," she says. "So they can sue you. That's why Cookie is honking the horn. You have to prove there was no malicious intent. Look at them, they're so . . . ridiculous."

She says *ridiculous* the way normal people say *rat* or *cancer,* with pure disdain. We pull away from the madness and head up into the Hills. At a red light, a couple in the car next to us look up and do a double take. They start waving and she smiles, says, "Whateverrr," under her breath. We pull away and the couple have a nice story to tell everyone at their next dinner party. We climb higher into the night, and she is skipping through tracks on the CD player now and rolling down the window, sticking her head out into the night and shouting to no one in particular, "Fuck!" Everyone in the car laughs and nods. They know exactly what she's talking about. The Disaster and I exchange glances from the backseat. She lights a cigarette and talks to the car about the house of Balenciaga or something, laughs loudly at some joke Cookie makes, calls her a "cunt." We bend around curves, the headlights illuminating the road ahead. We pull up to a gate that opens slowly, then we are inside. The lights in the house turn on automatically. No one is amazed by this except for the Disaster and me. Everyone piles out of the car and goes inside. More drinks.

She sits on the floor in the middle of the room, legs crossed, smoking a cigarette and talking about Damien Hirst's diamond-encrusted skull. She makes wild gestures with her arms; her voice is low and scratchy around the edges. It sounds as if it hurts her to speak, but she only stops when the mirror gets passed her way, then she ducks her head down and makes a few lines disappear. Her hair is long and straight and covers her entire face when she's snorting. When she's done, she knocks her head back and brushes the hair out of her eyes, laughs, and screams, "Oh, my Goddd." Her friends all laugh. Now she's at the stereo—what the rich refer to as "the entertainment center"—fumbling through some CDs, knocking stacks of them onto the tiled floor. She's shouting for Cookie to come help her find the Stooges album . . . "Cookie! Cooooookie, you cunt, where's the

Stooges?" she cackles. "Cookieeee! Stoooges!" She is out
of her mind. "Coo-kie!" she cries, then, silence, some
more rummaging, more shit falling onto the ground, followed by "Found it!" She walks away as *Raw Power* cranks
from the speakers at unfathomable volume, pulls open
the massive glass doors to her balcony, and dances out
into the darkness as Iggy wails about being a streetwalk-
ing cheetah with a heart full of napalm. She is shouting
and thrusting her middle fingers toward the heavens.
Judging from the looks in the room, this occurs fairly
regularly. Her neighbors must hate her.

I excuse myself from the room, and nobody so much
as looks at me, not even the Disaster, who is sunk deep
in an armchair, watching the show in disbelief. I wander
down the hallways, upstairs to another massive sitting
room, lined with leather-bound books, unopened, bought
for decorative purposes, with a fireplace filled with
candles, spatters of wax on the floor. "Gimme Danger"
is blasting downstairs, nearly drowning out her voice but
not *quite,* and I can hear her laughing about something
and squealing with delight. I go into an adjoining room,
this one filled with religious artifacts—a hanging cast-
iron cross, a book covered in golden Sanskrit—as if her
interior decorator were trying to cover all the bases. The
flat-screen TV on the far wall has probably never been
turned on; the remote and the manual sit on a glass coffee
table, still wrapped in plastic. I go into the bathroom for
no other reason than I can—I mean, how often do you
get to see a bathroom like this?—only it's clear this isn't
her bathroom, just one reserved for her many guests. You

can tell no one's been in here for a while; the medicine cabinet is empty, the sink is clean. This whole wing of the house is like a natural-history museum. I look at myself in the mirror and just smile. . . . *What am I doing here? How is this happening?*

When I head back downstairs, side two of *Raw Power* is already under way, only it's blasting to an empty room. Everyone has gone off to their respective corner of the house, to do whatever it is you do when you live in the guest wing of a celebrity's mansion (more cocaine?). The Disaster is gone too, which makes me chuckle a bit to myself. This kid from Florida, this wonderful son of the New South, is probably passed out in bed with a swan-necked model folded around him, a mirror on the bedside table, a mirror on the ceiling, smiling and snoring and dreaming big American dreams, the kind that aren't possible anywhere else but Hollywood. Tomorrow he will be bloated and red-eyed and hoarse, but he will still tell me all about his adventures, will spare no detail, will begin most sentences with "An' got-damn," will end them with a weary chuckle. He is perhaps the most predictable person I've ever met, the most dependable. You can set your watch to him.

"What are you laughing at," she purrs from the balcony, just as "I Need Somebody" is trailing off.

I smile and shrug. She beckons for me to come outside. I don't have any choice in the matter. The air is crisp, slightly cool. The lights of Los Angeles twinkle in the distance. She is leaning against the railing of her balcony, her amber hair flowing out into the canyon. She is looking right into me, biting the corner of her lip again. She is getting ready to sink her teeth into me.

"I think it's so cute how you little punk boys act like you hate girls," she jokes, lighting another cigarette. "It's like we're your enemies or something."

I tell her to replace *girls* with *everyone* and she'd be onto something. The whole night has been leading up to this moment, when we would be alone in the dark, her friends gone off into their own little worlds. It has been perfectly planned, a well-organized, businesslike seduction. You get the feeling she has done this before. She knows what she wants. She draws closer to me, her eyes looking up into mine, and she puts her hands on my chest, inching her lips closer, and then we kiss, and she bites my lip and pulls back, asks me, "Where are you sleeping tonight?"

It's a mere formality. She already knows the answer.

23

The sun is coming up but we're still awake. She lies next to me, in all her glory; the morning light is soft and blue and makes her skin glow. I want to trace the freckles on her shoulders into constellations. I want to map every square inch of her. She smokes a cigarette and looks up at the ceiling, casually stroking my leg, sighing. I kiss the top of her head to keep up the illusion. She keeps excusing herself to the bathroom and I know how it goes.

I fall asleep and have the most insane dreams. She shakes me awake a few hours later, her face hovering above mine. She tells me she's been watching me, says it was adorable. The ashtray by the chair backs up her story. I don't think she's slept—I don't know, she could have—and she's still as wired and lean as she was last night. She tells me we're going to a hotel, and I don't understand why, but I agree. I have to. I take a shower and put on the same clothes I wore the previous night. We barrel back down the hill in her SUV, and at least three cars are trailing us, photographers who accelerate around blind curves and try to overtake us, try to box us in. They dutifully fall back into line with the approach of oncoming traffic, then attempt to zoom ahead again when the road is clear. She is laughing and calling them "fuckers." It is the most point-less car chase I have ever been a part of.

We walk to the coffee shop in the hotel lobby, making our way through a wall of even *more* photographers, all of who seemed to know we'd be lunching here. She is care-ful not to grab my hand as we navigate past the lenses. Inside, we take a seat that's near enough to the window—a happy accident—and everyone in the place notices. They're all either blatantly staring at us or trying hard to make it look as if they were not. Either way it makes my skin crawl. I hide my eyes in the shoulder of her jacket. We sit next to each other—not across from each other—at a booth. Outside, the photographers trample the shrubbery to take our picture. She pretends not to notice. I can't do the same.

"Should we, you know, *move?*" I ask.

"It's fine," she says flatly, like I've let her down. Then she strokes my hair with her hand, laughs at nothing in particular. It is a great photo op.

I struggle to stay awake, but we're both so fucking out of it. She's high on whatever comes out of that little bag and goes up her nose in the bathroom. I'm just along for the ride. I am aware of exactly what we are, and exactly what this is. Business, pure and simple. A way to make the tabloids. "Who Is Her New Man?" the headlines will scream. If only they knew I'm just her man for the day, someone preselected to give her the *edge* her career needs. Her "rocker boyfriend," as the tabloids will put it. The waitress comes by and I order a ginger ale. I pull my hood over my head and kiss her neck to keep up the act. The hotel manager lowers the screens on the windows now, as a courtesy to her. It's feeding time at the zoo.

After lunch, we go up to her suite at the hotel. She has it reserved for all of infinity. I look around at all the furniture and mirrors and artfully arranged flowers and realize this is probably as close as I'll ever get to domesticity. She disappears to the bathroom again, and I follow her down the hallway, my feet padding on the cold wooden floor. Through a crack in the door I watch her shadow move. She runs the tap so I won't hear her snorting up the little lines. I'm not sure why she bothers with all the mystery. I already know exactly who she is. I think about leaving while she's in there, but I just can't bring myself to do it. I am fascinated by all of this, by her, because deep down I suspect she's just another sad, lonely girl. I think I can make her happy, can rescue her from her life and take her someplace far away. It is the hero in me. The ego. She turns off the tap and I slip back down the hall, sit in a chair and pretend to be interested in the latest issue of *LA Magazine,* which they always have in places like this. She walks into the room wearing only a bathrobe, traces her finger across my shoulders as she heads for the bedroom. She opens the robe a bit, and her golden shoulder peeks out of it. I dutifully follow her in.

She lies on the bed, the robe unfurled around her like a flag. Old Glory. I stand in the doorway and want to believe that this is going to be something more than it is.

Only I know it's not. She tells me she has condoms. It is like signing a contract. Initial here . . . and here. Notarized. Filed. One copy each for our attorneys. The hero in me dies a tragic death, as heroes tend to do. We complete a fruitful and successful business transaction while the photographers wait for us downstairs.

Later, as she sits on the floor by the bed, smoking a cigarette and talking to me about Transcendental Meditation (or, as she calls it, "TM") and how it "saved my life" or something, I get up and start getting dressed. She stubs her cigarette out and asks me where I'm going, and I tell her I've got to split. As I'm buckling my belt, she crawls across the room to me, wraps herself around my legs, looks up at me with hungry eyes, and purrs, "Sta-ayyy." I tell her I can't, that I've got to get back home, and I step through her grasp. You can tell this doesn't happen to her often. As I'm pulling on my shirt and walking out of the bedroom, she sits on the edge of the bed and pouts, legs crossed, then lights another cigarette.

"You don't have to do this, you know." She exhales. "You don't have to prove a point to me."

I tell her I'm not trying to prove any point, that I've just got to get back to my place. We both know that's a lie, but I can't stand being here any longer, trapped in this penthouse with her. I don't want to be a part of this anymore. I don't want to be pulled back down by her, don't need another addiction to (mis)handle. I'm heading out the door when she shouts that she'll call me, and then she cautions, "Leave out the back . . . it'll be easier that way."

I take the freight elevator down and exit the hotel

through the kitchen. A couple of Mexican kids in aprons are smoking out by the loading dock. As I walk by, they smile at me slyly. I'm probably not the first guy to leave this way. I walk a few blocks up to Sunset, call the Disaster, but he doesn't answer his phone. I hail a cab by a gas station and ride back to my place, making the driver take me back by the front of the hotel before we head into the canyon. Photographers are still out there, leaning on the hoods of cars, smoking cigarettes, drinking coffee out of paper cups. Their lives are one long stakeout. For the first time, I feel sort of sorry for her.

I try calling the Disaster again, but it goes straight to voice mail. He might still be at her house, asleep with a model wrapped around him and a smile on his face. But as the cab pulls up to our place, I see him on the front porch curled up in a wicker chair, asleep. I can hear him snoring as I walk up the dusty driveway. I kick a stone at the porch, but he doesn't stir. I shout his name . . . nothing. He finally wakes up as the cab rattles back down the canyon; a dry, sickly grin crawls across his stubbled face. He looks sunburned and ragged, as if he'd spent the day crawling through the Sahara. He's out on the porch because, last night, he lost both his keys *and* his phone.

"Ah think one of them girls musta taken 'em," he drawls, scratching his stomach. "Or maybe I lefem at th' house. You think we can go back there again tonight?"

I laugh and say that we probably won't be going back there anytime soon. As we go inside, he pats me on the back and chuckles, "Boy, whata night. . . ." I can tell he's aching to continue, but he knows that maybe right now isn't the best time to relive past glories. He is a good friend. The sun is slowly setting in the canyon, and the rocks are glowing electric red. We open the windows and sit on metal folding chairs—the only real furniture we've got in the place—listen to the birds settling into the trees for the night, greeting each other with their familiar calls. Soon the coyotes will emerge from their dens and scurry through the brush; the owls will start up their mysterious, sonorous racket. The moon will come up, will shine yellow on the canyon floor. She will still be up in our penthouse, alone, or with some other guy, it doesn't matter. I will still be sitting here, in this metal folding chair, with my best friend in the entire world. Maybe we will go out and explore, and maybe the Disaster will finally bag a coyote. Or maybe we won't. We've got plenty of beer and some great stories to tell, when the time is right. I think we both deserve a night in.

24

Pretty much everyone saw the pictures. People I haven't heard from since high school are texting me, my mom calls and tells me she doesn't approve, says she's read stories about that girl. I can hear my dad laughing in the background. Kids on message boards are talking about it, saying the usual stupid bullshit. I even get an e-mail from Her, a one-liner, "Star fucker," followed by a smiley face. The smiley face was key . . . otherwise I would've thought she was mad at me. Not that I cared or anything.

She is also calling me every other day, leaving me voice mails that are getting progressively more insane. At first, she was polite, rasping that she had a great time the other night, and if the Disaster and I (she calls him "your friend") want to come by the house again, just let her know. Received at 2:27 a.m. When I don't return her call, she leaves me *another* message, her voice a little more agitated, wondering where I've been hiding, what I've been up to. Received at 3:52 a.m. I can hear *Raw Power* playing in the background. When I *still* don't call back, she blows a gasket, leaves me a rambling message that says her cousin shot himself in the head, but he didn't die; rather, he'll be a zombie for the rest of his life. She says she'd call me bad luck, but I'd probably take that as a compliment. Received at 4:14 a.m. Worried, I finally call her back, ask about her cousin, and she sounds like she has no idea what I'm talking about. She calls me an asshole and tells me never to call her again before hanging up. Perhaps everything my mom read about her was true.

Our album is released and debuts. Heatseekers chart and all that. The first single is getting played on the radio, and our video is being shown on MTV (when they actually *show* music videos). The world is pulling me away from my hideout in the canyon, and I am obliged to obey. I pay the landlord six months' rent, and the Disaster and I rent a car and drive down to San Diego, where our tour is scheduled to begin. Meet up with the guys for the first time in months. Everyone is happy to see that I'm not only living, but *flourishing*. I joke that it's that good California air, and that they should all get the hell out of Chicago before it's too late. They all laugh. That night, we go out and get absolutely shitfaced in the Gaslamp; the Disaster and the Animal get into a brawl with a bunch of dudes from the navy. The two get beaten up pretty bad, but it wasn't a fair fight. The Disaster ices his face with a can of beer. The Animal swears a lot and says he's officially an enemy of the state. The tour begins the following night, at the decrepit, old San Diego Sports Arena. Before the show, the manager of the place excitedly tells us that Elvis Presley played there once and gave a brand-new

Cadillac to one of the security guys. We're more interested in the Chick-fil-A across the parking lot. We haven't
seen one of those since our swings down South.

The show is great, the kids are loud, and the place is
packed. I introduce a new song by shouting, "This one
is for anyone who's ever looked at their hometown *and
wanted to burn the motherfucker to the ground,*" and all the
girls squeal. I'm not sure if it's because I cursed, or because they hate San Diego. Probably a combination of the
two. Afterward, we hug each other and spray champagne
around Elvis's old dressing room. Our manager looks on
with a huge smile on his face. None of the other guys see
it, but he winks at me. We are off and running. We are
catching up to the present. We are in top form.

The tour snakes throughout the Southwest—Phoenix,
Flagstaff, Albuquerque, Santa Fe—and down into Texas,
skimming along the Mexican border (we campaigned
hard to take a detour into Juárez), shooting east to San
Antonio and Houston, a hard north to Dallas. The tour
bus slinks along through the night, taking us up into Oklahoma and Kansas. Our bus driver is a chain-smoking,
delightfully acrid road dog named Vincent, who used to
drive for Ozzy Osbourne and doesn't have time for your
shit. He stares out at the open road—the same road he's
stared out at a thousand times before—and tells us stories about Ozzy snorting just about everything you can
imagine, chasing women, and pissing on things, namely
the Alamo. "Shit, you guys are pussies compared to him,"
he sighs. He's probably right. We are stopping at Indian
casinos to play nickel slots, and places like Truckhenge,

outside Topeka, where a guy named Ron shows us the rusted-out trucks and buses he's stuck in the ground for no reason. Admission was free. Some nights we stay in hotels—each of us in our own room, finally—and terrorize the staff and our fellow guests. We toss furniture into the pool. Run the housekeeping carts down the hallway. Flush bizarre things down the toilet. Vincent drinks beer in the hotel bar and shakes his head. The following morning, the managers always give us dirty looks, but they don't say anything. I don't even have to use the business centers anymore . . . we've got wireless on the bus.

We head into Kansas City, two shows at a venue named after a cell phone company, then begin the long drive across Missouri (nothing in the middle except for Columbia). Hit St. Louis on a Tuesday and then head up into old Illinois, past Springfield and Decatur, heading home to Chicago. The show there is sold out, has been for weeks. My parents are coming, and so is my high school music teacher. Unlike at our last hometown show, she is going to be there too. I left Her two tickets and VIP passes at will call, just in case she wants to bring anyone. You know, Her roommate or whoever.

We get into Chicago a day early, and my parents take the Disaster and me out to dinner, ask us questions about California as if we've just returned home from a semester abroad or something. I will never grow up in their eyes. I am okay with that. After dinner, the waitress asks if she can take a picture with me. I laugh and pose for the shot, holding a goofy smile on my face while we wait for the flash to go off (the flash never goes off when it's supposed to). I glance over and see my mom and dad smiling. What must this be like for them? I am thinking, getting slightly emotional, when all of a sudden my dad sticks his tongue out and I crack up and the waitress and I have to take the picture again. My mom wraps up all the leftovers and has me take them back to the apartment, just in case.

My apartment is hermetically sealed. Frozen in time. An inch of dust is on everything. My bedroom is still filled with cardboard boxes, just like I had left them. Reminders of my previous life. I decide to unpack and put T-shirts I will never wear again into drawers I will probably never open again. It feels good to do it: I'm burying my past in a Hemnes dresser. I can remember the night she and I put it together, me getting all frustrated and Her trying so hard not to laugh. Her stuff is still in the bathroom, and I find myself staring at Her toothbrush, contemplating putting it in my mouth. It's almost as if she died or something. The Disaster is fumbling around with something in the living room, so I put the toothbrush down and turn off the light. I grab my coat—the one I had missed in New York—even though it's summer, and tell the Disaster I'm going to sleep at my parents' house. He doesn't object, probably because he knew I was going to anyway. My mom is so happy when she hears my key turning in the lock. We stay up and talk in the kitchen, then she touches my arm and tells me not to stay up too late. I sit there with the lights on, looking out the window, at nothing. Up the creaking stairs to my old bedroom, still there, still the same, not a speck of dust because my mom cleans it just in case I pop in unannounced. They have repainted my brother's room and put a treadmill in there. I think how pissed he'll be when he finds out and laugh to myself as I fall asleep.

The next morning, the Arts & Entertainment section of the newspaper has an interview with me. A full-color photo of the band. A mention of my infamous fling with you-know-who. My dad has left the paper open to the page, so when I come downstairs, I am greeted by my face staring up at me from the kitchen table. He smiles and asks if he can have my autograph. Then he tells me to mow the lawn. For the first time in history, I actually don't mind doing it. The big rock star, angling a Crafts-man mower around the flower beds. The Disaster comes by, and he and my dad sit on the porch and laugh at me. My dad is pretty close to retiring from his job at the law firm, so he doesn't give a fuck about anything anymore. He is sitting back in his chair, wearing jogging shorts and shoes with no socks, drinking a beer with the Disaster. He has raised two sons and has navigated his way through life. He has earned the right to have someone else mow the lawn for him. Someday I hope that will be me. Only I'll probably wear longer shorts.

That night, we play the Allstate Arena. Before the show, the manager presents us all with jerseys, our names stitched on the backs. I freak out way more than I probably should about this, and the manager looks at me like I'm crazy, but that's mostly because I'm so nervous. It's not that this is our hometown, or that my folks are going to be here, or even because *she* will. It's more about who she's bringing with Her. Doors are at 7:00 p.m. Kids start streaming in. Backstage, I am trying

unbelievably hard to stay cool. I walk the corridors in
my Columbia jersey. My parents come back to say hi,
wish me luck. My dad is drinking some champagne from
the craft-service table because, why not? My mom is
taking pictures of everything because she can. They are
having a ball. It's sweet, I suppose. The opening band
starts playing, and their guitars chase me back into the
dressing room. I feel the slight trickle of panic dripping down my spine. First time in months. I breathe and
count to ten. Let go of the moment. Try to remember
this is all beyond my control. Then there is a knock on
the door, and it's Her. I pretty much forget about all that
let-go-of-the-moment crap. The last time I saw Her was
when Her mother was sick, when I left Her apartment
and got on a plane headed back for Los Angeles. When I
was lost and manic and out of my mind. I can remember
Her kissing me with Her eyes bunched tight, still warm
and half-asleep, beautiful in the way all girls look when
they've just woken up. Now she looks *different*. Older.
The way exes always look when you see them again. You
notice the small things. She is wearing a jacket I have
never seen before. Her eyes are ringed and dark. We
hug and my face is in Her hair. She's still using the same
shampoo.

We make small talk: I ask about Her mom, she asks
about California. A wall is between us. Both of us want to
say something to the other, but neither of us have the guts
to do it. So we just shadowbox, pantomime. Then she tells
me she wants me to meet someone. The gloves come off.
The bottom falls out. We go out into the hallway and she

introduces me to Robert. "This is *Robert*," she says, raising her voice on his name, just so I know he's someone special. He is totally boring. Wire-rimmed glasses. Collared shirt. Dumb haircut. Small-dicked intellectual. He looks at me with a mixture of fear and jealousy, the way new boyfriends always look at the man they have replaced. He is picturing me fucking Her. Girls never notice these things.

"Hey," I say, and nod to him, and we shake hands, a gesture that never ceases to be awkward in situations like this. Then I just stare at him and wait for words to come out of his meager little mouth.

"Thanks for the tickets, man," Robert says, his voice rising slightly. He is way too excited. I can tell she is embarrassed.

"Sure," I say, hands on my hips. Then I am done with him, so I turn to Her. "Hey, can I talk to you for a minute?"

I pull Her into the dressing room before she can even answer. Robert stands in the hallway with his hands in his pockets. Frozen. The door latches behind us and I turn to Her, eyes wild. Part of me wants to throw Her down on the couch and remind Her what she's missing. Another part of me wants to cry. I feel so betrayed. So angry. I have no idea what is about to come out of my mouth.

"Are you *serious*?" she spits before I even have the opportunity to speak (she knows me pretty well by this point), then, again, just in case I didn't hear Her the first time, "Are you fucking *serious* right now?"

"You fucking bring a guy to my show?!" I yell, loud

enough so Robert can hear me. "I can't fucking believe you'd do that. Why would you fucking do that?"

"I'm not even going to fucking *talk* to you about this. I don't need to. We fucking *broke up*. I fucking *broke up with you*. I'm with Robert now, so what? Get over it. Grow the fuck up."

She goes to leave, but I grab Her arm. I pull Her close, just as I did the first night we met. I feel Her body against mine for the first time in months. It's not the same, but I'll take what I can get. I am out of my mind again. I want to ravage Her. I want to hit Her. Her eyes are wide. She is afraid.

"Look . . ." I trail off, not knowing what to say next. "Meet me later."

She pulls Herself away, leaves the room. I imagine Robert greeting Her on the other side of the door, asking Her, "What's *wrong*?" Being tender and supportive and weak. He probably wants to break down the door and break my neck, but he knows he can't. Not because he's too weak, but because my security guard is standing in his way. I wonder if they'll even stay for the show. I decide I don't care. Instead, I concentrate on getting incredibly, incongruously *drunk*. This is easier to do than you'd imagine, especially when you're the headliner on an arena tour. By the time we take the stage, I'm out of my head. I shimmy around the stage like an idiot. I climb my stack of amplifiers and leap down, crashing hard on the stage. I probably break something, only I don't feel it. The kids squeal and shout my name. My parents are watching from the side of the stage, backstage passes hanging around their necks, stupid smiles on their faces. I grab the microphone and dedicate the last song to Robert. The guys look at me like I'm insane. I am a terrible drunk, especially in Chicago.

That night, we have an after-party, at the same place we had our record-release party. The same place I got drunk and passed out in the bathroom and went home with that chick. She's probably here tonight, probably looking for one more opportunity with me. She won't get a chance this time because I am behaving myself tonight. Or at least trying. I keep calling Her phone because I want to hear Her voice, because I want to hear Her lips curl around the receiver. I want to tell Her about my plans of destruction. I want to be with Her. She doesn't answer, so I call back again. She says she's on the phone with Her aunt, and that she'll call me back, but I know she's actually talking to Robert. Nobody's aunt is awake at this time of night. I call back to confront Her with this fact, but it goes straight to voice mail. I leave Her a rambling message that's part accusation, part apology. Midway through, it occurs to me that I am still plenty drunk. I don't expect Her to call back—not ever—but, to my surprise, she does. She agrees to see me. I take a cab back to my parents' place, sneak my brother's car out of the garage again, and head over, even though I shouldn't be driving. I blast the radio and close one eye to keep the lines in the road from crossing. They do anyway, but I aim for the middle of the X.

I am too drunk to wonder why she's agreed to meet me, and I don't care. I just want to see Her. I pick Her up at Her apartment and we drive around the city for a bit, mostly because I don't want to take Her back to my place. It seems a bit forward of me. But I probably could because we both know exactly what this is. In the meantime, I try my best to keep the car on the road. I don't think I'm fooling Her. She is smoking cigarettes out the window. I ask Her what happened to Robert, the booze wafting out of my mouth in noxious purple fumes. She exhales and says, "It's just . . . he's . . . I don't want to talk about it." We don't.

We go back to my apartment, make more small talk ("You unpacked"), have meaningless, hopeless sex. Fake panting. She is thinking about me fucking you-know-who. So am I. We are both disappointed, both wanted more from this. But too much has happened now. We are too far gone. After, we lie in bed and I run my finger down the scar along Her spine. She is smoking and thinking about Robert. And what a terrible mistake she's made tonight. She falls asleep, and I lie there, staring at the ceiling. Eventually it gets too hot in my room, so I pull on clothes and leave. I think I hear Her wake up, but I don't stop. I walk around for what feels like hours, nowhere to go but only one place I don't want to be: next to Her. This was a mistake. I should never have called. I should never have ruined Her life again. Eventually, I call Her and she tells me she went home. Says the door is unlocked. Asks me what the hell is wrong with me? I tell Her I don't know, and she hangs up. When I get back, all traces of Her are gone. She even took Her toothbrush. But she's left a pack of cigarettes on the kitchen counter, next to my old medication. I stare at both for a while, decide to leave them where they are, perfectly placed, in memoriam. A few hours later our road manager picks me up, and we head back out onto the road. I didn't even get to say good-bye.

25

I sleep it off in my bunk. When I wake up, we're still driving, on Interstate 90, jumping off onto 94 toward Minneapolis. We play a show there that night, then follow the interstate up into the great stretches of nowhere, past Fargo, across North Dakota and Montana, where the country just becomes horizon for days on end. A succession of sunrises and sunsets with no obstructed views. God's country. You meet the mountains just past Bozeman, climb up into the clouds, your cell phone merely an afterthought at this point, a stop in Missoula, Wild West Cowboy College Town, then through Idaho within hours, into Washington, down into the valley, Spokane on a Saturday night. Across the great green expanses of the state, barreling down on Seattle, the glimmering emerald in the bosom of the mountains. Mount Rainier over our left shoulders. Then 90 expires, and we head down 5, along the coast, Tacoma, on toward Portland. Trees for miles, patches of bright red clay, God's dirt, the best there is. So clean and fresh, I almost consider shipping some back to the kids in the skyscrapers of Chicago, because they don't know what they're missing. Because words will never do it justice.

I love the long stretches between conversations best. The quiet is like blue waves running between screaming, tourist-filled islands. It doesn't feel forced; it feels okay to just be breathing, to just be riding up front with the guys, our little family band. I cool my cheek against the window, watch my breath fog the glass. At night the sky is lit with a million jumbled stars, scattered across sheets of velvet. The stars out West are jokes on city kids like me. They make you feel insignificant, they put you in your place. The rain and the fog are almost invitations to slip this bus off the road, into the trees, the sounds of glass shattering and metal bending, one wheel still spinning and the smell of pine cutting so hard. I'd be okay with dying in the woods just off Interstate 5.

There is nothing but days of driving now, a lull in the schedule. Oregon at a leisurely pace, National Forests around every turn. Into California, like another world up north, just redwood trees and mountain peaks. We are bound for Sacramento, the odd-fitting capital city, like Albany, only more depressing. It seems like an after-thought, something they decided to give the people there because all the good stuff had already been handed out to LA and San Fran and San Diego. A consolation prize. A show there and then two by the Bay and then home again for a few days, then flying out East to begin another tour, different bus, different driver, the same eternally shift-ing world. Our video is in the top five of *TRL*; we will be doing appearances in Times Square. Our album is selling more and more copies every week, and the label thinks that, with a second single, it will go platinum. We are a *priority* now. The shareholders have freed up more funds; we will be shooting another video, going to the UK and the rest of Europe. But all of that is still months away. Right now, we are stopped at a rest area outside Willows, California, sitting on the picnic tables out by the pine trees. Right now I look out at the traffic headed north, feeling the fleeting summer breeze on my neck, almost like a kiss or a caress. A wave good-bye. Right now I get a call on my cell phone, from a Chicago number I don't recognize. I answer. It's Her roommate. Right now she is crying on the other end of the line. Right now I hit the ground.

26

There was an accident. She was apparently driving drunk, hit a guardrail. No one knows where she was going. No one knows where she was beforehand. None of that matters much. She's in the hospital, a tube going into Her mouth, helping Her breathe. Tubes in Her arms are keeping Her alive. The remaining dates of the tour are canceled. I am on a plane bound for Chicago.

She's in the same hospital that Her mother was in, only a different wing. The bad wing. I tell the nurse at the desk that I'm here to see Her, and she looks at me with sad eyes. I take the elevator up with an orderly and a kid in a wheelchair. His stomach is distended with cancer. They get off on a different floor. I walk down the hallway to Her room, feel the sickly warmth of illness, the slightly sweet odor of feces. Hospitals always smell the same. I am numb. When I get to Her room, Her mother and father are there, Her sister too. They all look up at me, and you can tell they haven't slept, have been keeping vigil by Her bedside. Her parents are wondering why I am here, but they don't say it. Her sister asks if maybe they'd like to go get some coffee, and they begrudgingly say yes. Her father wheels Her mother past me, and she looks up at me with tired, angry eyes.

She was on the interstate when it happened, Her sister tells me. She has a lacerated liver and a punctured lung, massive head trauma. The doctors don't know if she'll ever wake up. Her head is battered and bandaged, turned to the left. Her eyes are both black. Dark red cuts peek out from beneath the gauze. The tube in Her mouth is held in place by tape. She looks so small and broken in the bed, Her thin arms resting at Her sides, black nail polish still on the tips of Her fingers. Machines surround the bed, whirring, hushed things, helping Her breathe. The dainty drip of the saline in the plastic bag. The chart hanging by Her feet. The thick hospital blanket tucked into the mattress. She is never going to wake up. She is going to die. Everyone knows it.

Her parents are gone for a long time, so I sit in a chair in the corner of the room, looking at Her bashed-in face, Her wondrous eyes tightly shut. Occasionally Her lashes flutter, but Her sister says that's just how these things go. She's probably gone already, she says, and we're looking at Her body. Her sister is brave. Braver than me when I was her age. Braver than me now too. A doctor comes into the room and looks at Her chart. We both stand up to greet him, and Her sister introduces me to him as "Her friend." I shake his hand because that's what you do in situations like this. Eventually, Her parents come back into the room, and Her father wheels Her mother next to the bed.

I give him my chair and stand by the window. No one says anything. The hours drag on. The curtains flutter slightly. Eventually, visiting hours are over, and I leave because I am just a visitor. I cannot offer these people any comfort. I cannot change the situation. I feel stupid and small. I can tell I'm not welcome.

I go back to my apartment and the Disaster is already there. The room is filled with awful silence. The kind of silence that only happens when someone dies. He leaves and comes back with a bottle of Jameson, sets it on the table, and we drink it in silence. Nothing can possibly be said. I wonder if this is what he did when his baby died. I don't say it because I already know the answer.

The next morning I am back at the hospital, sitting in the cafeteria. The room is full, but no one looks up from their table. I drink coffee from a paper cup. I wander the hallways, wondering how many ghosts are walking alongside me. I am putting off going to see Her because I don't want to see Her like this. For the first time, the thought occurs to me that perhaps this is all my fault. That she was coming to find me. I remember our last night together, how awful I was to Her. I cry in the chapel, say a prayer to God, who decided two nights ago that Her number was up. I go up to Her room, and Her family is still sitting there, only now they've multiplied to include grave-faced aunts and uncles and weeping grandmothers. I don't know any of them, and they do not acknowledge my presence. Because I have no place here.

The day goes on. Her sister and I have hushed conversations in the hallway about a funeral because Her mother doesn't want Her to hear us talking about death. We don't bother telling her that she can't hear us anymore. Her sister tells me that she always knew she loved me, and that she would be happy that I am here. Later, as Her family is down in the cafeteria, I sit with Her and tell Her how sorry I am for letting Her down, for hurting Her. She can't hear me. I watch Her chest rise and fall softly. Sometimes there are long gaps between breaths, and my heart pauses and a lump grows in my throat, and I'm begging Her to breathe again, and then she does, and everything returns to the way it was.

That night, as visiting hours are coming to an end, she is surrounded by doctors. Her family is crying and holding hands, telling Her they love Her and it's okay if she wants to go. She dies at 9:50 p.m. Wednesday, the seventeenth. No trumpets sound or angels descend. She just stopped breathing, and the machines went silent. She is already up in heaven or wherever, turning in Her time card. Maybe she is trying out Her new wings right now, afraid at first, but after a few tries mastering barrel rolls and graceful loops. That night, she doesn't come to me in my dreams, probably because she is too busy getting used to Her new accommodations.

The next few days are a blur. I tell Her father to call me if they need any help with any of the arrangements, but he never does. My parents send flowers. She is buried on a Saturday, but I can't bring myself to go to the funeral. In the morning, I had got dressed in my only black suit, but when I looked at myself in the mirror, I couldn't help but think that I looked like a giant phony. I couldn't imagine going through the motions, sitting in some church with my head bowed, listening to some priest talk about "the infinite wisdom of His ways" and "calling His flock home" and shit like that. So I didn't go. It's okay though, I don't think Her parents would've wanted me there anyway. My mom said it was a lovely service.

27

Still in Chicago. I spend my days in my bedroom, squinting my eyes and trying to make the shapes look like Her. It doesn't work. I spend my nights hoping she'll come see me, only she never does. I begin to think that maybe she's waiting for me to come to Her . . . after all, she was on Her way to me when she died. I wonder if killing yourself is the only thing you can control in your entire life, and that's why it's a sin. Because you're beating God at his own game.

I take the bottle of pills off the kitchen counter. Look at Her pack of cigarettes, still sitting there just as she left them. I smoke one in the living room because I don't care anymore. The sun is just breaking over the city, filling the apartment with soft white light. I take a cab to my parents' house, sneak my brother's car out of the garage, and start driving. I pull into an empty parking lot, turn the car off, and sit there for a while. She is in the car with me, I know it. I swallow the entire bottle of pills, sit back, and wait. I wonder what it will feel like. I turn on the radio.

When they find me, I want there to be music, and I want the car battery to be just as dead as I am.

Sometime around eight, things are getting hazy. I am lilting between this world and the next. My breathing is slow. My eyelids are fluttering. It feels like there are insects buzzing through my veins. Eight blue ones will do that to you. Her hand is holding mine, guiding me through to the other side. I am ready. But then, I get scared. I call my mom and mumble something to her. She is asking me where I am, what's going on, and telling me to drive to the emergency room. Somehow I turn the key, and *somehow* the engine starts, and now I am on the phone with my manager, and then the dangly-earring shrink in California, telling them that I want to die but can't bring myself to do it. I am crying and swerving all over the road. I love to hate attention. It's so predictable.

I tumble into the ER and they have me fill out forms. You should see my handwriting. They call my mom and then she is there with me, hugging me and telling me it's okay, hushing me as I sob. We sit in the waiting room, time dragging on into infinity. My mom laughs nervously. The thing inside my head bothers her far more than it bothers me. A fish tank is on the right side of the room, just between the bleeders. The fish are all a brilliant blue. I am mesmerized.

An old woman with a bandage wrapped around her head stands right in front of me, obscuring my view. She needs them more than I do. They call my name and take me into the next room. A security guard is by the door. He looks at me glumly. They say undress and put on the gown. I want to call Her up because she knows just how to get me out of my clothes.

"You can't have those in here," the guard says, pointing at my shoes. "The laces are considered a suicide risk."

I take off my shoes. The lights are bright and the door is open—nothing is going on here. I'm not getting away with anything. I ask the guard for a pen and paper because I'm bored and I want to write Her a letter. They are also considered a suicide risk and are denied. They make everything the whitest possible shade of white in the hospital. The lights are so white they burn your skin, or maybe that's just me imagining things. It makes me feel more alone than I ever have before. I am lying on a gurney that hundreds of people have died on. I lift myself off it quickly so none of their memories seep into me. I look around to make sure that no one saw me do this, no one saw me acting "crazy." The security guard is staring at me with the just-give-me-a-fucking-reason look, but settles back into the monotony.

The crisis counselor comes into the room and shuts the door, but she asks the guard to open the blinds and watch through the window. Now I am the brilliant-blue fish in the tank. The crisis counselor is a fucking amateur. If she had her shit together, I suppose she'd be in some nice building in the suburbs with a receptionist, not sitting here in a white cell, talking to me. She's out of her league with me, in too deep. I have read *The Pill Book* from front to back. I could talk my way out of anything. But I'm too busy swimming for the guard. She asks me why I'm here and if I've ever tried anything like this before. I know what *this* means. She jots my answers down on a pad of paper, sighs, and says she won't admit me to the hospital if I'll sign a contract saying I won't hurt myself. I actually laugh out loud at the thought that anyone depressed enough to kill himself would be stopped by a piece of paper. It's like slitting your wrists over a sink so you won't make a mess.

"I'm gonna have to go over this with my lawyer. And send back some markups," I joke. She doesn't laugh. Eventually she leaves the room and is replaced by a *second* counselor, a touchy-feely guy in a terrible sweater. He asks me the same questions, and it's getting difficult for me to keep my story straight. I feel myself bending it just to keep things interesting, adding bits about "God talking to me" and the like. He is nodding and taking notes. Then he looks up at me and asks why I wanted to hurt myself, says that someone "in your position" could make a difference. I tell him it makes no difference. I was proud of that one.

He leaves too, and I am alone in the room, the security guard watching me through the glass. I go over to the table and call the one person who matters, tell Her, "The Capulets and Montagues don't have shit on me and you." I am pretty sure I got Her voice mail. I call back and apologize for leaving the first message. I am talking into a phone that doesn't exist to a girl who doesn't exist anymore.

It turns out that I couldn't even kill myself the right

way. The medication takes time to get out of my system, so there is nothing else for me to do but sleep. My dreams are sterile and uninfected. I can't control the inside of my head right now. I feel paralyzed. My blood cells are pixilated. My pupils dilated. But I am alive. Alive and unwell. After three days, my parents come to take me home. No one talks in the car. My dad clears his throat. I sit in the backseat and stare out the window, at the last few moments of summer. Nothing will ever be the same again.

I float through a week at my parents' house like a ghost. My mom won't let me out of her sight. If I am in the bathroom for longer than five minutes, she knocks on the door and asks me if I'm all right. She doesn't understand that I'll never be all right, that it's beyond my control. She doesn't understand that I'm broken. A second week rolls in like fog. I go to visit Her grave. I stare at Her name carved in the granite, at the date of Her death. I don't want to leave Her but it's getting dark. I tell Her I'll see Her again, but I don't know when that will be. I want to die but just can't do it, no matter how hard I try. On the way back home, I call our manager and tell him I'm ready to tour again. I'm not sure why.

We have meetings. The guys are concerned. It's only been two weeks, after all. I tell them I'm fine, joke that I didn't even punch a mirror this time. I tell them that I need this, that I am drowning in Chicago and want to get back on the road. I am lying but they believe me, and the tour is scheduled to resume in a week's time. A doctor will be traveling on the road with us, "just in case." I leave

Chicago and fly to Philadelphia, pick up where I left off. The first few shows, I am tired and weak, and the guys have to carry me through the set. Kids hold up signs with my name on them. I tell them that I love them all.

The tour heads south, through Jersey, into DC. The shows aren't getting any better. I can't be bothered to try any harder than I already am. Everyone knows this is a mistake, but they're all afraid to tell me. I'm too fragile. They are finishing this tour *in spite* of me. At night I lie in my bunk and wonder if tonight will be the night I get to see Her again, but she never visits. She probably can't forgive me. I am so tired but I can't fall asleep, so the doctor teaches me an old trick—try to be perfectly still, close your eyes, and attempt to locate the sound of your pulse. It may take a few minutes, but you'll hear it, it will be there. It will grow stronger. It will envelop you. You will eventually fall asleep. Sometimes it actually works.

Maryland rolls by, Virgina, the Carolinas. Such great sadness. Cities stop mattering. They are just names on a spreadsheet. I check them off one at a time. We head through Georgia, and I begin taking girls back to my hotel rooms. Meaningless sex to fill the void. We shoot down I-95 to the Disaster's hometown of Jacksonville. His parents and brothers come to the show that night. They all look like fatter versions of him. He is beaming and showing them around backstage, pointing out all the guitars that he's in charge of, picking them up and tuning them as they watch in rapt silence. It makes me think of that show back in Chicago, when I grabbed Her and frightened Her.

I want to go back to Her grave and apologize. But there's no time. There never will be.

We cut across I-10, long stretches of swamp and nothingness. Alligator farms and air force bases. Through the great, sweaty South—Interstate 10 is a dire road. Show in Mobile, along the Gulf of Mexico. It never ends. I miss Her and she is never coming home again. It is beyond my control, and I have resigned myself to that. Someday my number will be called, and all I can do is hope she'll wait for me up there until it is. I am not optimistic about my chances.

We leave Mobile in the middle of the night, bound for New Orleans, on the brown banks of Lake Pontchartrain. The guys are screwing around in the front of the bus. I am in my bunk, trying to sleep. I press my head against the pillow, close my eyes, and listen for my pulse, but the engine is too loud. We barrel through the darkness. The road hums beneath my head. The wind whistles against the window. Eventually, my heart stops racing and I drift away.

Somewhere in Mississippi, I can feel Her floating above me. I open my eyes and she is there, inches from my face yet still miles away. Infinite space and time are between us. Her hair is long now, the color of honey, and slowly waving in the night air. Her eyes are greener than they've ever been before, like pastures after a rain, and Her skin is the purest white. She glows softly in the dark, magical and ethereal, like lightning bugs in a jar. Just out of reach. She is the first ghost I've ever seen, but

I am not afraid. I want to feel Her on my fingertips one more time. I want to tell Her that I love Her. But I am afraid to move or make a sound because I don't want to frighten Her away, so I just lie there. She understands, and she smiles down upon me. Everything else falls away. I close my eyes and mouth the words I can't bring myself to say. She can read my lips. We head toward the sunrise, together.

ACKNOWLEDGMENTS

This book and much of my (in)sanity would not be possible without: My dad for inspiring me to follow my own course in life, my mom, brother and sister: Andrew and Hilary, the tireless believer in me and single greatest supporter of *Gray*: Bob McLynn, Jonathan Daniels, Lauren McKenna, Ryan Harbage, James Montgomery for making sense of me when even I couldn't and getting it right—for bringing this book back to life multiple times. Leslie Simon, CRUSH, Simon and Schuster, my friends in Chicago and around the world, my brothers in the band, and to the single greatest journey of my life: Bronx Mowgli Wentz.